RIEDEN REECE AND THE BROKEN MOON

Published by Mindfast Publishing

3245 University Avenue Suite 1132, San Diego, CA 92104

Visit the author's website at www.authormattguzman.com

Cover by Kim Dingwall; Edited by Stephanie Slagle; Author photo by Donald Carlton

ISBN 979-8-9865098-0-8 (ebook) ISBN 979-8-9865098-1-5 (paperback) ISBN 979-8-9865098-2-2 (hardcover)

Library of Congress Control Number: 2022918386

Publisher's Cataloging-in-Publication data

Names: Guzman, Matt, author.

Title: Rieden Reece and the broken moon : book one / Matt Guzman.

Description: San Diego, CA: Mindfast Publishing, 2023. Identifiers: LCCN: 2022918386 | ISBN: 979-8-9865098-2-2 (hardcover) | 979-8-9865098-1-5 (paperback) Subjects: LCSH Extraterrestrial beings--Fiction. | Human-alien encounters--Fiction. | Science fiction. | Adventure fiction. | BISAC YOUNG ADULT FICTION / Science Fiction / General Classification: LCC PS3607.U986 R54 2023 | DDC 813.6--dc23

First Edition: January 2023

10 9 8 7 6 5 4 3 2 1

Printed in the United States of America

Krystal —

Be authentic and yourself. You are really enough just the way you are. :)

RIEDEN REECE

AND THE REECE

BROKEN MOON

BOOK ONE

MATT GUZMAN

MINDFAST PUBLISHING

Contents

For my beloved grandma and mom. My grandma inspired my love for science fiction. And my mom inspired my love for storytelling.

A speck
on a speck
on a speck.

"Ideas, dreams, beliefs and hope. Only a fool believes life might be anything more than that." – The Atomic Protector

1

The Mysterious Moon

I T ALL STARTED WHEN the moon cracked.

Ri had already been having a tough day. Earlier, after school, he'd ridden his bike home, lost in thought. He had forgotten to avoid riding down his small town's most dangerous street: Star Cactus Lane. When he wasn't distracted, he could predict the future. Use his superior understanding of the world to anticipate what might come next. Not today.

The three bullies—intent on tormenting him—jumped out of the alley and threw sticks at his tires. He swerved like a maniac and almost crashed. Heart pumping and legs shaking, he biked home in record time. He tossed his bike into the bushes, rushed up the steps, and swung open the door. He flung his backpack across the living room, and it crashed into the couch. He slammed the door with all his strength and opened his mouth to curse the bullies.

His mother jumped and spilled her hot tea on the dining room table. She sat in the dark, her face buried in her right hand. Her dirty blonde hair hung in sweaty strings across her small shoulders. She kept her head down. "Rieden," she mumbled. "Why are you so loud?"

Still struggling to catch his breath, Ri snapped back, "Sorry, Mom. I thought you were still working at the hospital."

Ri kicked off his shoes into the corner. Ri's mom gripped her tea with one hand and rubbed her temple with the other. "How was school?"

"Fine." Not fine. Never fine. School: a form of torture invented by sick, twisted people with a craving to ruin people's lives. Wasting his time memorizing dead people's birthdates was a pathetic use of his superior intellect. But Ri never told his mom the truth. She wanted to pretend life was a carnival. *Well, kids get sick at carnivals too, Mom. The rides make them sick. The candy makes them sick. But sure, let's pretend it's all fun and games.* Still, the urge to protect his mom from his personal problems with bullies trumped his wish to come clean. His mom needed him to be strong, for them both.

His mom sipped her tea. "Probably not fine, mister."

She used a certain tone that smacked him hard. He rushed over to the kitchen and switched on the light. "Why are you sitting in the dark?"

His mom covered her eyes and blocked the light with her hand. "Stop! I've got a headache. Turn it off."

Ri shrugged his shoulders and shut off the light. "Whatever." He shuffled toward his bedroom.

His mom rubbed her temples with both hands, hovering over her teacup with her eyes shut. "No video games until you do your schoolwork."

School. The bullies. His mom acting weird. It all exploded in his head. He shouted way louder than he intended, "Leave me alone! I get straight A's and always get it done. Why do you tell me what to do? Stop bugging me." His explosion came out of nowhere, and he regretted it in an instant. He tried to make it to his room before his mom could say anything. Her sigh trailed behind him. He had disappointed her—again.

So, yeah, it hadn't been a great day. And now, to add to his list of problems, he had lost his knack for sleep.

He tried pulling the covers over his head and counting sheep. The sheep refused to stay in their pen. Those feisty little troublemakers would jump out and scamper in aimless directions. He chased them, but they pretended not to listen. "Ugh!" He grabbed the sides of his pillow and squeezed until his fingers throbbed. Nobody listened to him. Such was the sad life of a thirteen-year-old.

The heat from his blanket layers made him sweat. He used to sneak a light under his blanket at night and read his favorite novels. Not anymore. Now he craved sleep, and the sheep disobeyed. And his mind replayed his argument with his mom. A skipping record. Same argument, same reaction, on repeat.

And then everything got so much worse.

The bed started to shake. He figured the family dog, Bess, was scratching behind her ears. Her vigorous scratching often shook the foot of his bed. Except, the shaking continued. It shook harder and longer.

This is...not normal, he thought.

His bed banging against the wooden floor played in harmony with the pounding of his heart. He swallowed hard and waited; the deafening roar pounded his eardrums. He lay frozen in place, unable to move. The banging refused to stop.

He waited with bated breath for his mom to race into his room and check on him. She would grab his hand. Scoop him from bed and help him escape the shaking.

She never came. Nobody came. He lay there, alone. He tried to yell out for his mom, to check on her—the cry stuck in his throat.

Earthquake.

The shaking lasted so long, soon his heartbeat calmed down. He needed to do something. Only weaklings lay in bed and waited to die.

He peeled the blanket away from his face and gasped. The light blinded him.

He blinked several times, adjusting to the bright light. The source of the light poured in through his bedroom window. The moon. Brighter than he had ever seen it before. And huge! It filled the window frame from edge to edge. And the blue! The moon never shone so bright. Was he making things up? Was it morning already and this was really the sun?

No. For sure, the moon.

And it vibrated. He dropped the covers to his feet and swung his legs over the side of his bed, gaping at the moon. The cold air tickled his toes. He didn't bother searching for his slippers. The brilliant moon's glow reeled in his full attention.

He crept to the window. The cold wood against his feet sent shivers up his spine. When would his mom come running? The moon vibrated! And glowed a bright blue light. The entire house shook, and he imagined the entire planet did too. The end of everything rattled his bones. What a beautifully terrifying way to go.

The moon stopped shaking. And it grew larger, filling the sky. Then it shrank. It reminded him of a star turning supernova. Then it did one more impossible thing.

The moon cracked.

Ri's jaw dropped. A jagged lightning mark cracked downward, close to the center, yet veered to the left. And not completely in half—two-thirds of the way down. A left chunk of the moon shifted sideways.

The moon hung there limply in the sky. Broken wide. Defeated. Done.

The shaking stopped. The brilliant blue light disappeared. The moon shrank to normal size.

Ri squinted up at the night sky. The explosion of light had given him temporary night blindness. The moon appeared fuzzy, and he needed a clearer picture of what was happening....

Duh! He raced to his closet for his digital camera. His dad had sent it to him, and it lay buried in the back. The Canon D-30 came with an extra zoom feature. The moonlight reflected from the full-length mirror attached to his closet door. After a moment of digging through his messy closet with scattered broken toys, he found the Canon. He ran back to his window and peered through it. He focused on the moon.

Wait. What? His eyes popped open wide. Was that a...a giant *hand* coming out? The crack remained.

Ri's grip trembled, and he almost dropped the camera. He squeezed it so hard his knuckles turned white. He zoomed in for a better inspection. Sure enough, a large hand emerged from the crack in the moon.

His heart hammered and his temples throbbed. His mother had never prepared him for cracking moons and hands crawling out. No, this was fine. Everything was okay. The moon was far away. The hand couldn't reach him. Correction—the arm and hand couldn't reach him.

His thoughts raced at full throttle. He stared through the camera lens at what emerged from the broken moon.

The arm became a torso, became two arms, became a head. The head's features remained hidden. Only a shadow outline of a tall, thin humanoid figure. He had read so many alien-invasion books, enough to believe one might really happen someday—but this challenged his imagination. His rapid thoughts tripped over themselves.

His breathing burst out fast and shallow. Dizziness consumed him. No. No. No falling apart now. He needed to stay strong for his mom. Pay close attention. Find out if the human-shaped shadow crawling out of the moon was a friend or an enemy.

The entire human form pulled itself from the crack in the moon. It sat with careless effort on the edge, its long legs dangling back and forth. Its shadow feet scraped at the nearby stars. The motion blew bits of starlight glowing and fading into charcoal embers. The mystery human figure seemed larger than the moon. Could he be dreaming this? Ri slapped his face three times. The only thing that changed was his stinging left cheek.

The figure bobbed its head around. It hopped down, hanging from the jagged moon crack with its right hand. It swung back and forth—a bored monkey. It leaped to Earth.

And disappeared.

Ri's jaw clamped shut, crushing his teeth. He lost track of the shadow. It blended into the darkness. *Where did it go?* How far away did this danger loom? This strange night twisted every known fact about size, physical laws, and dimensions. His understanding of the world he thought he knew was crumbling apart. Nothing had prepared him for this moment.

Somebody else might've questioned their own sanity. Another thirteen-year-old boy might've concluded they were dealing with a fever or even hallucinating. Not Ri. He trusted his brain. His intellect hummed with flawless perfection. The best part of his personality involved his superior cognitive ability. He could always trust his brain—what he saw, what he thought, what he understood.

Yet now, his brain grinded to a halt.

He dropped the camera to his side, squinted into the night, and scanned for the shadow. He needed to warn people. People couldn't ignore a shadowy figure the size of the moon with the power to crack it. He considered calling 911.

He prided himself on his one positive talent. Predicting the future. Foreseeing events before they happened. His therapist—Esther

Evans—had warned him such thought processes created anxiety. They reinforced his fears. Therapists pretended they knew everything. They couldn't climb inside his cranium, though. His future predictions often came true. If he called 911, they would laugh at him. Adults never believed him even when he told the boring truth. No way would they believe him now. They'd hang right up, call him a liar, tell him to stop wasting their time telling made-up stories.

He had a mission to find evidence. A mission to chase the shadow.

A memory gnawed at him. A reminder. A familiar thought whispering from the back of his mind. The crazy cracking moon took over his thinking. It gripped him and he lost focus.

He shook away the mental cobwebs. Time to act. Time to crush his fear. He channeled his younger nine-year-old self. The version of himself who'd saved his classmate's life by sprinting to get help. He needed to find proof. A shadow on a picture from a camera proved nothing. Anyone could create a fake pic.

A noise outside his window halted his barefoot pacing. He recognized the familiar noise. Someone had stepped on the old garden hose and pulled on the outdoor hose bib. The hose bib bounced against the watering can.

Someone was creeping through his backyard.

Ri glanced at his Men in Black wall clock above his bed. 11:30 p.m. Bess slept inside the house, tucked into her doggie bed within the soundproof room. She wouldn't hear it there. No barking.

His pep talk dissolved into a churning sea of bile burning up his throat. The shadow. He sensed the shadow's presence. His mind told him to look out the window, but his body refused to obey. He didn't have to look to know for certain.

The shadow human was sneaking around his backyard.

He stepped backward away from the window until his closet door stopped his retreat. The cotton fibers on his pajamas caught on the door's rough surface and held him in place with the strength of Velcro.

He clamped his mouth shut and held his breath. *Be quiet. Don't draw attention to yourself.*

Silence.

Stillness.

Loud ringing in his ears.

A hand slammed against his window.

2

The Shadowy Soul

R I CLAPPED HIS HANDS over his mouth and suppressed a scream. He peered at the window with wide eyes. The shadow man's oversized white gloves pushed against the glass. The pressure caused the glass to bulge.

A hundred thoughts raced through his mind. *Run. Freeze. No, run! No, protect your mom. Face the man. Run away and he'll chase you, not your mom. Run. Freeze.*

A white glove formed a fat fist and knocked on the glass pane. *Rap. Rap. Rap.*

The two hands drummed on the window with all ten fingers. Then another impossible thing happened—the two hands pushed through the glass. They didn't break it. They didn't open it. The white gloves slid through the windowpane like it was air.

The shadow man passed through with a slow calmness. A window with no more substance than falling water in a shower.

"Who—what are you—" Ri started, so surprised he didn't know what to say.

The shadow man tripped on the solid window sill and fell headfirst into Ri's bedroom, stirring up a loud racket. He addressed the wall with a booming voice, "Ah, yes. *That's* it. I've now cracked how to uncrack it."

Ri jumped forward, untangling himself from the closet door. "Shh! You're being too loud!"

The tall, lanky shadow man jumped, and his limbs bounced in awkward directions. He moved with the dexterity of a poorly assembled jigsaw puzzle. He adjusted his colossal straw hat and wiped his forehead with an oversized white glove. "Well, well, well. How about *you're* too quiet."

"You're in my house and making a racket. Breaking the moon. Sneaking through my backyard. Walking through walls. You gotta keep it down. You'll wake my mom and what am I supposed to tell her? She'll never believe me!"

The shadow man placed his gloved hands behind his head. "Okay. Inform me what you consider too loud. Is this too loud?" His jaw dropped to his belly, and he screeched out a blaring horn from a freight train. The wind blew Ri toward the closet door, and he fell hard across the attached mirror. He strained against the force of the tornado to cover the shadow man's mouth—the wind overpowered him.

Ri shouted, "Keep it down!"

The shadow man obeyed and projected the grin of a rare clown who enjoyed being a clown. Such an unnerving expression. Ri didn't have time to shudder, though; the hallway light switched on and streamed in through the gap under the bedroom door.

In a mad frenzy, Ri rushed to the shadow man. He pushed him toward the space under his bed. "Quick! Hide! It's my mom!"

The huge humanoid creature crouched next to the bed, completely failing to hide any of its body.

Ri scrambled into bed and jerked his blanket over his head. He hoped his mom wouldn't open the door. Sometimes she turned on the light to warn him. His body trembled.

After a few minutes, which stretched out into a painful eternity, the light switched off. His mom's bedroom door closed with a soft whisper.

The blood returned to his face and ignited into a fire. He whipped away the covers. He scowled at the odd and awkward intruder—a confused crouching animal. "What is wrong with you! Why are you here? Who are you?"

The shadow man raised a padded finger. He reached up and adjusted his massive straw hat. The hat realignment manifested a faint roar—like firework rockets flying. Ri winced, his eyes flicking toward his closed bedroom door again.

The shadow man's surreal eyes bulged for a flash and focused. Ri was still waiting for an answer, and he had a bunch more questions he wanted to ask this invading creature. Like how exactly he had come through Ri's bedroom window without breaking it, what he wanted with him, and why he had destroyed their moon. But the hat trick stirred his curiosity. And Ri's curiosity calmed his goosebumps. Instead of the logical questions, he asked, "Did you somehow turn up your intelligence? When you moved your hat, your eyes got way smarter looking."

The shadow man puffed out his fluffy chest. The edges of his straw hat brushed the ceiling rafters. "Intelligence? What an astonishing word. Why, no? Or yes? Adjusted my position in your universe. I arrived slightly...off? Not on? Not sure, your words here are limiting and foreign and incomplete."

Ri sat cross-legged in bed and studied the curious creature. He resembled a crudely drawn cartoon. Or a toy. Or something else unreal. "Are you a friend or a stranger? You made quite the entrance. How and why did you break our moon?"

The shadow man pointed toward the starry sky. His painted eyes flattened into two slits. "Hmm. I wish to answer your questions, but the words are not forming. I sense gaps. Allow me to readjust further."

The shadow man lifted a gloved finger. He studied the window and stared for an uncomfortable length of time. Like a shutdown robot. Then he snapped his fluffy white gloves. He seized the window latch with the eagerness of a monkey discovering a banana. Opening the latch, he lifted the window. He squeezed his oversized body into a sitting position on the ledge.

He unwedged himself and tugged on the window's sides. Somehow the window grew bigger. A simple change with the ease of someone clicking icons on a computer screen. Ri's eyes widened in awe. The shadow man pulled the window several times until it doubled in size. He clapped his huge hands. He sat his giant frame on the enlarged window trim and kicked out his feet. He rested a stick elbow on the top edge of the fish aquarium.

Ri tightened his slack jaw. "How did you do that?"

The shadow man's painted face stared him down. One eyebrow lifted into his hat, the other one dropped to his nose. "Searching for the word. Alzheimer's? Amnesia? Ampersand? Did you not observe my entrance? I impressed you with a simple cognitive alteration?"

The vein in Ri's forehead throbbed when older people spoke advanced words. They meant no harm, he knew; they'd lived extra years to accumulate extra words. Regardless. It tasted rude. Worse than those annoying people who chewed gum with their mouth open. He could usually figure out the advanced words' meanings from their context, but his therapist told him he had parapraxis. Sometimes his words would get jumbled when he tried to repeat them aloud.

"You're not answering any of my questions. You're a guest in my house. Not invited. You're a trashpasser."

"Trespasser."

Ri slammed a palm across his forehead. "Gosh. You're so annoying. Answer one question. Something. Who are you? What's your name?"

The shadow man gripped the sides of his straw hat and lifted his chin. He spoke at the ceiling while peering downward with bugeyes. "I am the Great and Powerful One and Only Director of All and Bringer of Knowledge to Universal Harmony with Strength of the Atomic Protector."

"Um. Okay. Yeah. Do you have, possibly, a *shorter* name? What if we're going on an adventure and we run into some danger? Spouting off a long sentence like that to grab your attention seems dumb."

"Interesting. I've told you so little. You speak of adventure. How do you perceive this?"

"Duh. I can predict the future. It's obvious. Now, shorter name? My thinker keeps calling you Shadow Man. Pshaw, what an awful name."

"Hmm. Shadow Man. Fun. It does kind of fit."

"No! Only if you're a bad guy! A bad guy lurks in the shadows. Are you saying you're a bad guy?"

The shadow man stretched his oversized glove to stroke his painted chin. He motioned with the care of someone wiping fingerprints from a bowling ball. "All these misleading concepts. Good, bad. So basic. I mean, for a four-year-old, okay. How old are you, thirteen? Nobody is all good or all bad all the time. Those are judgments based on moments. I can behave badly if I choose."

"Is that why you came here? To do bad things?"

"No. Not particularly. Oh, I skipped over information. Your flow of time in this universe is so dreadfully boring. It's straight and predictable.

No wonder people hunt for distractions. Here." The shadow man extracted something from within his straw hat—a hidden light source. An old-fashioned scroll. Small, with dimensions similar to a paperback book.

The shadow man cleared his throat in an official manner. "Ahem. Yes. By the decree of me, I do summon a helper. A keeper of knowledge and summoner of universal power. One to watch over, protect, lead, or support based on the necessities required. This one is destined to help me find what we lost. This noble pursuit supersedes all other priorities. I sacrifice everything unnecessary or arbitrary to accomplish this purpose. He shall stay by my side, with deep respect and autonomy. Also, with friendship and love, until I recover what we lost."

A long yawn escaped Ri. The pre-adventure stuff sounded boring. Maybe he would snag some sleep, after all. "Um. Nice speech, I guess. You wrote that?"

"Me? How flattering. A kind compliment. No, no. *You* wrote that."

Ri blinked in astonishment. "What? What are you talking about? You must be confused. Are you at the wrong address? You bothering the wrong Rieden Reece? No way I wrote that."

"Well, of course, you retain no memory of it in this universe because of the boring and predictable flow of time. You did write those words at some place and some time."

Ri twisted his mouth, still not believing him. He attended Horton Middle School. His English teacher, Mr. Coldbell—an odd, short man with a bald head and a wicked temper—gave him some advice once. The advice? Dismissing truth, because you're afraid to believe it, is dangerous. Believe it first, until proven wrong. Or something along those lines. The point: he refused to believe he had written that scroll.

But what if he had?

He bit his lower lip. He chewed on the words, not willing to admit his complete lack of understanding. "So, sometime in the future, I summoned you to help me find something I lost? Did I get it right?"

"Yes. Good. Not bad. You understand."

"Er, what did I lose?"

The shadow man cracked open his painted mouth and shut it fast, holding a gloved forefinger high in the air. "Ah, yes. Well. It's unclear. *That's* what makes it an adventure."

Ri slapped his forehead and shook his head. So many questions bubbled up, and the shadow man had answered none of them. Exhaustion crept up his body and weighed down his thoughts. "Whatever, shadow man. We're *not* going on an adventure at midnight. I need sleep. And if my mom finds you here, I'll be grounded until I'm eighteen. Go ahead and push yourself back out the window and go sleep in the desert under the moon you broke. We'll plan your annoying adventure in the morning." With that, Ri jumped into bed, pulled the covers over his head, and ignored what the shadow man said.

Ri hid under the covers, waiting for silence. The hard pounding of his heart shook his entire bed.

3

The Missing Mug

I N SPITE OF HIS exhaustion, Ri tossed and turned all night. He wrestled with the weight of his crushing thoughts. The broken moon. The shadow man. Something missing in the future. None of it made any sense. And those type of problems swirled and swirled around the cesspool of his anxiety. Counting sheep provided no relief. Those pesky sheep would put on their reading glasses and pull out their calculators. They tried to help him solve his problems instead of jumping over their stupid gate.

His eyelids launched upward when a giant white glove shook him so hard his teeth clattered together. "What! What! What!"

The shadow man glared. "Please exercise caution during your sleep cycle. Shifting realities. If you attain a certain frequency, you can slip into an alternate one and wake up with different details. Your consciousness will remember the incongruities."

"What? What are you babbling about? Shifting realities? Is that because you broke the moon?"

The shadow man shrugged and lifted his two gloves. "I'm not an expert on humans or your universe. Your minds are constructed in a curious way. Sleep accesses the baseline fabric of the universal flow." His calm reply sounded like he was talking about the weather.

Adults had the bad habit of explaining complex subjects in a way that made zero sense. So did aliens. Ri itched to find answers, but asking this alien questions was getting him nowhere. He needed a new tactic.

Ri rubbed his eyes and grumbled. "I hardly slept, obsessing over this ridiculous adventure. At first, it sounded fun. Now it's becoming a whole bunch of work. Reminds me of schoolwork. And not the fun kind where you build a toothpick bridge. The boring kind where you memorize dead people's birthdates and similar garbage."

The shadow man patted his straw hat. "You're disagreeable in the morning. And surmising, at other times too. This will lift your spirits. I've etched out a better name for myself. Carved out a bit of starlight. Please ascribe to me the name 'Rozul.'"

Ri yawned. "Rozul? Weird. What does it mean?"

"Mean? It means my name. What you call me. The formation of funny sounds you force from your face."

Ri's jaw unhinged, poised to argue. The opportunity to express his retort left.

The bedroom door flew open.

He almost shouted at—Rozul—to hide. Rozul loomed too large, but the door opened too fast. He decided, instead, to analyze his mom's face and figure out if she appeared mad or scared. That became a befuddling problem.

His mom had no face.

Where her normal head should've been was a floating ball of black darkness. Inside the ball of darkness, lightning and a strobe of sparkling dots twinkled in and out of existence. It resembled a planet, made up of a tiny universe, replacing the space her head occupied. Ri's lower lip quivered. He tried to push his mouth open to say something. To speak to her. To ask her what was wrong. The words stayed frozen in a lump caught in his throat.

His mom with a black hole for a head stood in the doorway. She refused to enter. She refused to leave. She poised herself there stationed with annoying parent patience. He fumbled to locate some words. He turned to ask Rozul a question—Rozul solidified into a statue. A powered-down, silent robot.

Ri hammered his fist into his pillow. This often disturbed his mom, yet now she didn't react at all. She stayed mute. His logical mental processes tripped. The butterflies in his stomach performed somersaults. He struggled to find a single word to say, something to maintain their precious connection.

After a crushing string of seconds, the space-head version of his mom closed the door. He strained his ears to hear her steps echoing down the hallway.

Rozul broke his statue stance. "Whew. Things are changing fast. We must move this adventure along, with a pronto surge of speed."

Ri tamped down his urge to cry. Parents claimed with hollow arguments that crying was okay. Crying never made him feel okay. It made him weak. A little baby. Crying meant you failed. It meant you stank at being a good person. Crying left you weak and open to an attack by bullies. Never cry. Never cry.

The image of his mom with her missing head burned into his brain. A single tear birthed in his left eye. It dangled on the edge, ready to race down his cheek. He coughed too loud. "Um, so, did I do that? Did I sleep us into the wrong universe?"

"No, not quite how sleep-slipping works. Hard to explain with the inadequate words you call language. It's difficult to explain what *exactly* is happening. There are unavoidable consequences for tapping into a universal source without authorization. If it's anyone's fault, it's mine. I came here in a hurry. No worries. We can fix all with time."

"Fixed? My *mom's head is a black hole!*"

"Unfortunate."

"Unfortunate! Why? Why is my mom's head a mess of universal space?"

"Not sure. One problem, one solution."

Ri formed fists and shook them at his ceiling. "Ugh! It's worse than talking to a girl! You're making zero sense! I thought you could give me answers. Why did you come here? So far, all you've done is break our moon, and now you've broken my mom too. I can't take this anymore!"

"What did you expect?"

"Not this!"

"Well, you expected wrong. It happens. A lot. No point in getting mad. Let's direct action toward the task for which I came."

Ri grabbed Rozul's stick wrists. A mysterious calmness soothed his skin. His blood pressure sizzled. His body ached from lack of sleep. He drifted through thick fog. The moment he touched Rozul, his emotions evaporated. A raging forest fire retreated into two pilot lights burning in his heart. Quiet calmness enveloped him.

He released his grip. The calmness remained, and he clenched his powerful fists. Powerful star energy flowed through his veins, electricity sparking along his skin. The spectacular buzz from drinking a hundred energy drinks.

Rozul provided no commentary on Ri's change in emotions. Ri itched to find answers, although he kept the calming reaction to himself. "What's the plan?"

Rozul danced his gloved fingers. "You make the plans. I'm here to help."

Ri shrugged. His infused calmness prevented him from overreacting. "Well, okay. Fair enough. Do we know what we're seeking? No. We gotta figure that out first. So, since we need time to think, I'm going to school."

During the process of readying himself for school, he skipped steps. He forgot to floss. He forgot to put the cap on the toothpaste. He forgot to comb his hair. He left both caps off his contact lens holder. His mom always scolded him for not focusing on the present task he performed. This morning's distraction loomed bigger than his previous problems. It consumed his full attention.

He slipped on his old torn jeans, his school sneakers, and his favorite lucky shirt. A dirty wrinkled red t-shirt with a faded picture of his favorite band, Muse. He swung his Marvel backpack over his right shoulder. "You can't follow me out the front door. Stretch the window again and meet me outside."

"Nobody can see me except you."

Ri pursed his lips. "Uh-uh. I'm too smart for this. Tell me the truth. Have I lost my mind? Am I imagining this? I've read stories of people suffering from hallucinations and other stuff. Are you for real, or am I talking to a whacked-out version of myself?"

Rozul crossed his arms and patted his shoulders with his gigantic gloves. "There's a flaw in your question. If what you propose is true, I'm the last person to answer your question definitively."

Ri poked Rozul's thin wooden leg. His leg retained the texture of a tree with no bark. Smooth, strong, and warm. There was no way for him to prove or disprove what Rozul had told him. He could only wait to see what happened.

He shrugged and opened his bedroom door. He tiptoed down the hallway and peeked into the kitchen. His mom and her black bowling ball head were washing dishes. She faced away from him. A bowl of cereal waited on the table, though he refused to go near that a-mom-anation.

His favorite therapist, Esther, had taught him mindfulness of his fear flare-ups. In this moment, he lost the ability to control himself. He raced past the kitchen. Vaulting through the open door, he sailed down the steps.

The loud, lumbering footfalls of Rozul followed close on his heels. Ri slammed the door, expecting to hear his mom shouting after him. He heard nothing. Apparently, she was indifferent to him now.

He typed in the four-digit pin for his bike chain lock and ignored the hunger grumbling in his stomach. And then it hit him, the thing that sent a shiver of unease down his spine.

Silence.

A force muffled the constant din of the world. He dropped the lock and examined his neighborhood. Mr. and Mrs. Whitman walking their two Labrador Retrievers. Mr. Juliano driving his old Buick down the street. The little dinky park across the way that his mom had nicknamed Fenway. Three mothers pushing their strollers with babies. A small strip of green where cart vendors sold coffee and breakfast on a stick. His neighbor Grace Alden pulling weeds in her front lawn. Dave—the mailman—strolling down the sidewalk. Their silence wasn't the only unnerving thing.

Ri's jaw dropped, and the blood rushed out of his head. He staggered backward and grabbed his bike to hold him steady.

Each person's neck supported a black ball universe instead of a human head.

4

The Candy Cheeks

H E PEDALED HIS BIKE fast while Rozul jogged beside him. A lumbering clown floating through the air with each gigantic step. A foolish grin was painted on his plastic face.

Ri's heart raced faster than he could pedal. "Dude! Shadows. My town is *trashed*. What is happening? Why has everyone lost their head? Are you *sure* it's not because I slept us into a different universe?"

"No. Same plane of perception, all the details track, and the vibration is correct. This is different. Something I've never encountered before. Such occurrences happen within infinity, of course."

Half panting, half shouting, Ri mimicked and mocked Rozul. "Of course. Of course. My big broken mystery! What's the point of you being here? This is all your fault."

"Quite possible." Rozul rotated and ran backward. He leapt backward with long steps, almost in slow motion. "I'm not responsible for your anger. That's your choice."

Ri grumbled. Rozul reminded him of his therapist, Esther, with her constant verbal corrections. He squeezed his handlebars hard, draining the blood from his knuckles. Part of him wished he were only imagining all of these bizarre happenings. That would solve his problem of having no plan to fix the broken pieces of his world. Rozul had broken his universe in ways that defied logic. Asking questions about it landed him nowhere. He needed to stop blaming and start finding solutions.

The school bus passed him on the right at the same moment he hit a patch of soft sand. He fumbled the bike for a couple pedals but recovered and kept it steady while the school bus sped away. The kids on board displayed normal human heads, pimples and all.

Ri shouted, "Well, at least we didn't break everything!"

A few minutes later, he skidded to a stop in the parking lot and ran his bike up to the rack. He whipped off his chain wrapped around the stem of the seat and locked his bike in place.

He leaped backward and almost knocked over Shelly Sanderson. Shelly. An annoying girl who talked too much and played nice with him and pretended they were friends. She stood with her hands planted on her hips. He suspected Shelly hoped he might ask her out. He'd only recently discovered reasons to tolerate girls. And he preferred Lisa Lemmons. Lisa laughed the loudest with the most infectious smile and didn't act dumb.

Shelly annoyed him, especially when she breathed. On most average days, he would feign kindness. Not because he chose to. If he didn't, his spineless teachers would tattle on him. They would call his mom with complaints, insisting Ri was "acting out again." To keep his mom off his back, he'd made the decision to tolerate Shelly.

Today, he reached absolute zero for patience.

Shelly twisted her right index finger around one of her brown curls. "Rieden. You're 'riding' too fast!" She giggled.

Shelly chose to pronounce his full name with a long i instead of a long e. The only preference Ri had for how others pronounced his name was not pronouncing it at all. It took him a moment to digest her pun. Ri would've picked drinking jalapeño juice any day over listening to puns.

And he was pretty sure jalapeño juice was disgusting. "Uh, yeah, lots on my mind."

Shelly perked up. "Oh? What's on your mind?"

He furrowed his brow. "Um, yeah. You know. Boy stuff. Gross boy stuff that'd make you sick." Rozul lifted his big gloves high, waving for him to hurry. Ri shrugged him off.

Shelly motioned her head at the next building. "We should get to English class—it starts in five minutes. Want to walk together?"

He almost burst into laughter. *No way!* He almost spoke the words, not caring that they would hurt her feelings. If the class tattletale, Brian Bowman, caught him walking with Shelly, he would never hear the end of it. Ri suspected he might skip school anyway. How to pull off ditching school under the radar? Adult spying eyes and ears surrounded him. Well, not anymore. Now, he needed to thwart the spying black circular balls of space.

He jerked his thumb backward. "I've got to go catch a lizard, kill it, and dissect it. Wanna help me?"

Shelly wrinkled her nose and shook her mound of curls. He caught sight of something peculiar. Her cheeks glistened extra pink. Not slightly pink, blushing from a pale-skinned girl's embarrassment. Bright cotton-candy pink. Instinctively, he plucked the thin sugary fibers comprising her cheeks. He pulled and the cotton candy ripped free. He sifted the fibers between his fingers, and they dissolved into sparkles of fine dust.

Shelly slapped her cheek and screamed. Ri wondered if the cotton candy fibers he'd pulled from her face caused her pain. Her eyebrows smooshed together in embarrassment though, not pain. A gravitational energy pulled on his left side. Mr. Coldbell stood there, pointing. Ri recognized the ugly tan sweater. If Mr. Coldbell spoke any words, Ri didn't hear any of them. The black sphere of space hovering above the teacher's neck filled with silent, flashing lightning. A group of kids paraded by and paid no attention to Mr. Coldbell's sphere space-face. Did they not see it, or did they not care?

Shelly burst into sobs and ran away. Mr. Coldbell towered near him, silent, pointing. Ri had no clue what the teacher was trying to say. He fumbled to hold on to reality within his skewed perception. He ignored the teacher and plodded in the opposite direction. Out of the corner of his eye, he spotted Brian Bowman waddling toward him.

"Come on, Rozul. Brian's trying to catch me, and I'm in no mood to tease that goober-head today." He sprinted to the far end of the football field near the big Palo Verde tree.

It took a minute for him to catch his breath. He leaned against the intertwined tree trunk and crossed his arms.

Rozul, the towering giant, grabbed a branch and swung from it back and forth, his knees scraping the dirt. "What's wrong?"

Ri squashed his urge to lash out at him. Wasn't it *obvious* what was wrong? The smart area of his brain remembered his tiredness, hunger, and stress. He initiated the breathing techniques his therapist had taught him.

Afterward, he unfolded his arms and poked his finger into Rozul's chest as he hung halfway down from the tree. "You're not telling me everything."

"Of course not. No one can tell you everything."

"Why do you do that? You spit out gibberish. What I mean is, you're connected to vital information. We have zero clues. I'm lost. Nothing makes sense. What am I supposed to do?"

"Whatever you choose."

Ri squeezed a fist and shook it. "You said we're on an adventure. You said I summoned you from the future. You said I've lost something. Is it adults' heads we've lost?"

"We seem to have lost those, yes."

Ri threw his arms up into the air. "Look! Rozul! You need to help me out here. You can't even answer my basic questions. It's alien invasion 101. Where did you come from? Are there more of you coming? How did you get here? Why did you break the moon? Can you answer one question? Your dumb scroll said I lost something. What did I lose?"

Rozul reached beneath his straw hat and retrieved the small scroll. He lifted it up to the sunlight and peered at it as if deciphering a hidden invisible word. He rolled up the scroll. "It doesn't specify. I'm wondering..."

"Wondering? What?"

"Well, have you ever lost a memory? Misplaced it, I mean."

"Um, well, you make it sound like a toy. You mean, something you forgot and should remember?"

"A memory is a thing. It's made and stored in your head. Sometimes you lose it. And if you lose a memory, you're unable to remember what you lost."

"What's your point?"

"I've lost a memory. Or more than one. Maybe, maybe that's the reason why I'm struggling to help you."

Ri's chest heaved for a second in response to the curious creature. In cracking the moon, something unintended had broken off Rozul. An interesting connection synapsed within the smart part of Ri's brain.

He slapped his forehead. "Of course. Of course! That's it. *That's* what I lost."

Rozul let go of the branch and stood up. "What? What did you lose?"

"You said it. I've lost a memory!"

"Wait. Pause. We've *both* lost memories? Yes. Okay. Wait? Isn't that what I suggested? I'm confused about your current excitement with my idea."

"No, listen. You're not listening. Don't steal my thunder—this is *my* idea. You're only halfway there. I'm guessing you lost a memory on purpose. My future-self sent you back withholding answers. My present-self must need to figure it out, because if my future-self tells my present-self, then I won't figure it out. Duh, the same thing happened in that one movie."

Rozul's brushstroke eyes swirled. "Your logic is perplexing."

"Don't you see? It all makes sense. I mean, nothing makes sense. That's why. Because I've lost my ability to remember. If I remembered what I lost, all this crazy stuff would make sense. Our memories are connected. We are somehow connected in the future. So, our memories must be connected. Don't you see? Don't you see?"

"We're searching for our lost memories?"

"Yes!"

"Well, where do memories get lost in your world? Where do we quest?"

Ri furrowed his brow and clamped his jaw shut hard. *Where, oh where?* A puzzling question. He kicked the dirt. Where in the world would they find a memory?

Rozul tapped his hat. "Okay. I found something. A library? Are you acquainted with what a library is? According to my language matrix, a library is a place where humans store their memories."

"Ah! Makes sense. Okay, we'll find a clue at the library. Let's go there now."

Rozul waved a glove in the direction of the football field and school. "Do you not have an important appointment? You mentioned we needed to hurry so angry adults could shove useless information down your throat. I'm still not clear on how that form of learning works. A form of eating, I presume—"

Ri cut him off. "Not important. Are you joking me? Did you see the teachers' heads? Nobody is gonna care if I skip school. And besides, if those adult monsters are still aware, then I'm already busted. They'll send me to the principal's office and call my mom again for making Shelly cry. Zero time for that. We gotta figure out what's going on fast so we can fix the broken moon. And the messed-up adults. And my mom. Who knows how much time we have?"

Mentioning his mom reminded him of the worst part of all this. The memory of his mom missing her head flashed in his mind, and it tugged at his heart. His chest ached. He needed to fix the universe fast, for her sake. No matter how much they fought, his mom meant everything to him. He couldn't imagine a world without her in it.

Rozul rubbed his chin, swirling the paint with his gloved finger. "Yes. Your logic is *not* perplexing. Humans are an unpredictable sort of creature, are they not?"

Ri shook off the pain and focused his mind on finding solutions. He jumped forward and sprinted across the football field, waving at Rozul to follow. He skidded to a stop and winced. He'd just remembered one important thing.

The librarian *hated* him.

5

The Cross Curator

R I AND THE TALL, awkward alien stood at the entrance to the Pioneer Desert Public Library. A tired old building slumped into a street corner down the block from his school. Rozul adjusted his hat. "Curious."

"What? What's so curious about a boring library?"

"No. Not this ugly antiquated architecture. These fortress pillars at the entrance are equipped with advanced technology. Scanners beyond humans' current development. It suggests an alien technology. And my language matrix supplies this phrase: Librarian of Death. Does that word combination mean anything important?"

Ri studied the empty parking lot and the library entrance. The two old tag sensors seemed worn-out and broken down. What was Rozul babbling on about? "Librarian of Death? Hmm. Well, the librarian here hates me. She caught me stealing books last year and has had it out for me ever since. It's not my fault there are rules about how many books you can check out..."

Ri trailed off. A thunderbolt idea lit up his mind. "Hey. Wait. Could aliens be here already? Hiding? I'm thinking the librarian who hates me is an alien, your Librarian of Death. Sounds about right. She seems like the kind of person who would have kids buried in her backyard."

Rozul's limbs shuddered. "That image makes me scared out of my nitwits."

"Come on. We're wasting time. Let's get in there and search for a clue. Nobody is at the library at this time of the morning. It could be a good thing the librarian is an alien. If she spots you, maybe it won't bug her. We need to run inside fast and hope nobody sees you."

By a stroke of luck, the librarian had left the front desk. A Lorax High School kid sat at the desk. High school students sometimes volunteered to help at the public library for class credit. The kid glanced up as Ri raced inside, his backpack a wounded bird flapping wildly in the wind. He etched away a mental note: the older teenager possessed a normal head. He also didn't show any sign of seeing Rozul.

Ri skidded around the corner into the history section. He caught his breath, keeping his mouth open wide to silence his panting. He yanked on Rozul's popsicle stick arm. "What are we looking for? A book? Something inside a book? A portal? Any idea?"

Rozul adjusted the books on a shelf near him, pushing some in, pulling some out, turning some forty-five degrees. He rolled his cue ball head sideways, and a bulging plastic eye bobbed up and down. "We're searching for our lost memories."

Ri dropped his backpack to the floor and ripped open the zipper. He rummaged through his stuff and mumbled, "A memory is in the brain. We're not looking for pieces of brain. You gotta save it. A memory file on a computer saved onto a drive. The memories are saved somewhere. Hidden. In a unique way. You follow?"

Rozul pulled three random-sized books off the shelf and juggled them effortlessly. "Your words translate, although your meaning doesn't. I'll choose to trust you. You have this figured out."

A small child—a girl between eight and nine—turned the corner. She made eye contact with Ri, not acknowledging the gigantic, fabricated figure juggling books. Rozul refrained from freezing into statue-mode, yet she paid him no regard. These moments made Ri question his own sanity.

The small unsupervised child lingered. Probably a homeschooled kid dropped off by her irresponsible teenage sibling so they could go do something shady. The child showed no signs of leaving. Ri bared his teeth and growled. The child's eyelids flipped up high and she scurried away.

Ri shoved his fist through the juggling space and knocked the books down. Rozul gawked at the pile of crashed books with painted star eyes. "That seemed unnecessary."

The familiar heat burned across Ri's cheeks, his heart rate increased, and a bead of sweat formed on his brow. The anger he worked so hard to fix for his mom flared up with regular familiarity. His wasted time attending weekly therapy sessions and disappointing Esther. "Hey. Shadow Man or Rozul, whatever. I'm fond of you, even if you're kind of annoying. But you're not focused. You're not helping. We need to locate our memories, and we have zero leads for what we're even hunting for."

"What makes you believe I'm not helping?"

"Um. Juggling books. Distracted. Playing. Not helping."

Rozul remained undeterred. He bent down, picked up the three books, and resumed juggling. He juggled and instructed. "Patience. You should not rush this process. Pushing harder doesn't make things go your way. Not with people, anyway. People are slow, they think slow, they believe slow, they grow slow. At least, people in your world. You asked me to help with finding our memories. I'm helping."

Ri parted his lips to protest; he gave up. So many of the things Rozul said equaled zero sense. Still, Ri adapted quickly. His gut told him the odd alien was performing something important. What that importance might mean, he hadn't the slightest clue. He could wait. If this was what Rozul needed to do to find answers, then Ri would accept that. Ri had nothing. No memories, no idea how to find memories.

Rozul juggled the books—tiny flapping birds within his giant gloves. He snagged a fourth book and fed the blurry circle. He lumbered, moving without a sense of urgency—like an ant wading through molasses. Yet, when he seized the next book, he moved almost at the speed of light, faster than the human eye could track. He added another book. And another book.

The books increased in speed. The roaring wind echoed through the library. Ri expected the death-dealing librarian to stroll around the corner at any second. Would she retain her head? Would she see Rozul?

The spinning books vibrated with mesmerizing speed. The books whirled faster and faster. Rozul's hands blurred into fan blades spinning too fast. He dropped his gloves, and the books continued to rotate with autonomy. Electricity sparked within the circle. Sapphire smoke drifted inside the swirling sphere. He controlled the spinning cloud with invisible strings. The inky void disappeared into an infinite point—a tornado vortex.

Ri shouted over the roaring wind, "What is it?"

"An energy-filter. It burns away the smoke of fabrication. Come here, view the bookshelf through the porthole."

Ri gazed through the whirring window of spinning books. A new, unfamiliar clarity opened his rigid mentality. The process resembled an optometrist examination. Without contact lenses, he fumbled through a blurry world. Peering through the lens machine sharpened the world into full focus. The bookshelf remained a bookshelf. The books shined clear. Crystal clear. His judgment of ordinary books changed forever.

He let out a held breath. "Why do the books look the same and different? It's extraordinary. Fascinating."

"Observing commonplace things from an unfamiliar perspective can jar belief systems. If you spend your life attached to one way of seeing, life is dull and boring. You only experience existence through your perspective. The perspective you choose can flavor your views and enhance your hues."

Ri grasped the invisible strings controlling the smoke-filled window viewer. He sauntered through the library and examined the shelves through the whirring lens of spinning books. Some of the books shuffled. They appeared alive. The words sparkled and vibrated. The colors shifted. A few of the books grew teal tentacle smoke hands that reached out to grab him.

He ignored the subjects and sections. He strolled down all the aisles, mesmerized by the living words dancing in rhythm. One of the aisles framed a small pile of half-eaten books. Book spines collapsed into a discarded mound of bones from a vicious predator.

He stumbled into the disaster relief section. The books on the shelves vibrated and danced in a humming harmony. One book in the center glowed with bright moonlight. It pulsated, cerulean liquid dripping from the shelf. He fixated on the book.

He slid the book off the shelf. He touched it, and the same calmness Rozul had transmitted earlier soothed him. Except, this book had one slight difference—it buzzed and hummed with happiness.

He pulled the book close to him; it appeared normal. He placed it behind the spinning window, and the book almost smiled at him. The title: *Emergency Preparation for Libraries*. He placed it behind the portal, and the title changed to: *Emergency Preparation for Memories*.

Memories. Their new mission. Rozul had helped him again.

Ri waved the book around with the enthusiasm from scoring the winning touchdown. "I found it! I found it!"

Rozul touched the portal of spinning books. The books stopped spinning, brakes on a car screeching to a halt. The books collapsed and crash-landed with a loud, echoing bang. The roaring wind dulled to nothing, enhancing the deafening silence of the library.

Ri's forehead creased. "Why'd you do that? Your porthole changes the book into something special."

Rozul leaned against the shelf. "I'm tired. Takes too much energy. Digging for wisdom takes a shovelful out of me."

Ri wrinkled his nose at the regular book. He desired the clarity of reality via the spinning lucid window. Still. He treasured the book. It contained their missing memories.

"Okay. Let's get outta here..." The rest of his sentence fell into the abyss.

From around the corner emerged the evil librarian. Minus her head. The black sphere of electricity crackling above her neck burned with intensity.

For a moment, the odd alien stood there, appearing unshaken. He remained steady, calm, and reflective.

Then Rozul screamed, "Run for your life!"

6

The Black Book

ROZUL ERUPTED WITH AN unexpected burst of energy. He grabbed Ri by the scruff of his collar and pulled him away from the frightful librarian. Ri's feet hardly touched the ground as he peeled down the aisle, racing opposite the silent woman.

He caught sight of her reflection in a mirror. Her black hole head had grown to three times its normal size. She lifted her hands, and bolts of electricity snapped between them and her black hole head. A bolt of lightning exploded from her fingertips. It cracked through the library and showered sparks next to them.

Ri sprinted through the fortress pillars with his precious book tucked beneath his armpit. He refused to check out the book. His mom would call his action stealing. He knew better. Only a temporary borrow until he could recover their memories.

"Hurry!" shrieked Rozul as another shower of sparks rained down on their heels, just as they neared the library's entrance.

Once outside, Ri climbed back onto his bike and rode off, Rozul right beside him. He pedaled for a mile before he dared to survey behind him. The library and its ominous guardian faded into the distance. He sputtered a laugh. "Wow. Man. So super close. She almost caught us."

Rozul bounded with immense strides next to him. "The crack in your world is spreading fast. Too fast. I should've anticipated a Guardian

Inspector would defend our hidden memories. This cloaked curator is an extra strong one. She almost stopped us. This adventure is more dangerous than I expected."

A discombobulated Rozul disturbed him. Rozul was supposed to be his rock. Strong. Confident. Determined. Hearing him verbalize his fears sent an icicle shiver down Ri's shoulder. He shook his head. "I don't understand. If she's a powerful alien, how did we escape so easily? Why didn't she follow us outside? And why did she have a black hole head like all the human adults?"

"I'm guessing her human cloaking device was affected in the same way the other adults were. She is guarding many secrets and may not want to abandon them to chase us. A Guardian Inspector is a patient role. We must be careful and not throw caution to the window." Rozul slapped his enormous glove against Ri's back. "It's okay, there's a reassuring 55 percent chance we'll win."

Ri gaped. "55 percent? What? Those are horrible odds!"

Rozul placed a fluffy finger on his plastic nose. "I would think those are tremendous odds. After all, most situations in life are 50/50. Either they'll happen or they won't happen. An extra 5 percent? I'll bet on those odds."

Ri almost repeated his mother's words, *"We don't bet, son."* 55 percent? A failing grade. He changed the subject. "Give me more intel on this Guardian Inspector. Will she follow us? Report us? Call my mother?"

"Doubtful. The fact the GI is there means we're being interfered with. Someone from your future timeline is tracking our plans. It means we're required to proceed super-duper carefully. Act only with extreme caution. A GI is powerful, though not the most powerful, of course."

Ri despised the evil librarian. Last year, his favorite librarian had retired. This new abhorrent replacement had shattered his opinion of librarians. Before her retirement, he'd assumed librarians swore a solemn oath to uphold the role of loving, giving, and special people. Become beautiful souls with only one desire to spread precious words.

Nope.

When this new librarian had caught him stealing books, she made it into some big drama. Worried his delicate mom. Made the situation seem like he was some hopeless delinquent. Now that he knew the librarian might have been an alien all along, it made perfect sense. She sensed his brilliant ability to see through her self-righteous attitude. She was a fake. A fake human hiding secrets.

His legs burned from sprinting and hard pedaling. The road he followed converted into soft sand and followed the train tracks. The last street at the south end of town near the tracks had a couple dozen abandoned houses. Ri's favorite abandoned house with overgrown salt cedars rested on the corner. His mom had forbidden him to go there, but it would hide their activity. It remained clear of any space-head adults.

He skidded his back tire sideways and jumped off his bike. He ran it along the right edge of the house under the canopy of green and brown needles. The rough ends scratched against his forearms.

Rozul shook the branches while wading through the low overhang. He stretched up his glove and combed the needles. He laughed out loud.

Ri leaned against a mammoth branch extending from the trunk of the tree. "What's so funny?"

"Old Salt Cedar told me a story."

The novelty of ridiculous things happening wore off. "Oh. I see. You talk to trees."

Rozul plopped down underneath the low canopy and displaced a heap of needles and trash. He reclined on one long, skinny arm, lounging for a picnic. "Your words are not precise enough. Talk? Implying the use of rushing air through vocal cords to produce vibrations? No. Communicate. I can communicate with all living cells in your specific spectrum. It is fascinating and fun. In my world, I am an elementary being. In your world, I am superior to most."

"Whoa, bro. Definitely not a humble thing to say."

"Hmm. True. Simply stating my fact of being to my trusted friend. If I used my superiority to harm others, especially for my personal gain, I could see the impropriety."

"What makes you *so* superior? That's a subjective belief."

"Ah. Not enough context, I conclude. Forgive me, your language in this plane of existence is limiting. I'm not superior to others in value. I bear the superior ability to communicate with all life forms. In my original plane of existence, smooshing thoughts into words via language has been dead for millions of years. I can communicate there. The oldest of our kind can communicate with much more benefit and beauty than I could hope to express. All intelligent life retains the same intrinsic value. Though some of our people have studied and focused on communication for longer than I've been alive. Am I getting closer to providing you with the correct perspective?"

"No. Zero sense, Shadow Man. So, what story did the tree tell you?"

"She told me her life story. It's much too time-consuming to translate into words. There's one way to share, if you're interested." He stretched his fluffy glove forward, palm up.

Who cares about some dumb story involving an abandoned tree? Ri almost rolled his eyes, but when he thought about the tree, a memory from his past whispered to him. He tried to grab the memory, but it slipped away. He lost hold of whatever it was the tree had reminded him of.

He quieted the churning in his stomach and waved the outstretched glove away. "Forget it. We'll waste time on stories later. I do want to hear more about where you came from, why you're here, and why you busted our moon. But one thing at a time. Getting our memories back from this book is the number one most important thing. How do we open this book? Why's it so heavy?"

The book appeared small and standard. Yet it was way too heavy, threatening to slip right out of his hands. It mimicked a gold brick; the size implied a lighter weight. He opened the cover and flipped through blank pages. The cover displayed no title, no writing.

Rozul approached the book cautiously, as if it were a dangerous snake. "It's encased. That's a protective shell. You crack open the egg? A safe? Something with cracks, a sidewalk? My, quite strange words here."

"Are you done babbling, crazy alien? Should I break the case off or something?"

"Yes! No. Not sure. Refrain from damaging the real book inside."

Ri flipped it over, struggling with its weight. It fooled him with the deception of an optical illusion. The pitch-black cover soaked in stray light beams seeping through branches. It reflected absolute zero back. Staring at the cover made his stomach acid churn. The book's smooth texture slid across his fingers and tingled his skin.

He slapped the cover. "Can you bring back the window juggling thing you did in the library? Studying it through portal view might give us a clue."

"Not possible. Every book stored in that special library is a portal into a new world. Weaving together the power from many books in new combinations creates a new point of view. I can only forge the coding lens inside the library."

"Heat? Cold? Force? Special words? Move the book to a specific place? There are a hundred things we could do with zero time to waste. How do we crack the code?"

Ri gripped the heavy book with his two hands, holding it up to the tree. Scraps of sunlight and moving shadows from the swaying branches danced across his hands. The dark shadows reminded him of his poor mom. Standing there in his bedroom doorway. Her head gone. Helpless. Unable to see or hear him. He wanted to blame Rozul, but blaming him wouldn't fix anything. Ri's amazing ability to predict the future screamed a loud warning at him. It screamed from the back of his mind and shook his body. Time was running out. He needed to find answers. And this book. This book was the key.

The crackle of rocks on pavement created by a slow-moving car interrupted them. A cop or a nosy neighbor? Ri had hidden his bike in a hurry; he hoped no one could spot it from the road. He held his breath and strained his ears—the tires crawled along the old road. A few seconds later, the car sped away.

He bit his lower lip, the hanging mystery threads tugging at him. And still, Rozul was just standing there, useless. Ri fought back the urge to scream. "Argh! We gotta fix the broken moon! The adults' heads! Our entire universe! Despite the fact you can talk to trees, you can't rip this shell off our book hiding our lost memories. One second, you're spouting *all* the answers. The next you sit there dripping dumb looks from your face!"

Rozul picked up a pile of dead needles from the dirt and tossed the pile into the air. The needles drifted down around him with the comfort of soft falling rain.

Rain. Water. Wet. An idea crystallized, and Ri's face lit up. "You've got it! That's it. You've cracked the code."

Rozul shrugged, brushing needles off his straw hat. "I did? What did I crack?"

Ri leaped into a run. "Come on. Let's go! There's an old canal next to the train tracks. We're gonna soak this book in water—water is the key!"

A plastic grin cracked along Rozul's curved face. "I'm a genius."

7

The Slippery Solution

R I GROWLED AT THE submerged book. "What a dumb idea."

Rozul whispered at a tall weed on the other side of the dilapidated canal. Another ginormous weed grew from a crack in the crumbling cement, blocking his view. He shrugged. "My conclusion is you're ruining all the invisible words on the paper."

"Thanks. Thanks. You're always *so* comforting."

Rozul beamed, oblivious to the sarcasm. "Yes, truth, although painful, can provide much comfort."

Ri snatched the book from the murky water. Because of the smooth frictionless cover, it slipped from his hands. He batted at it wildly. He smacked it with such force, it flew forward and smashed into a rock by the canal. It slid backward near the water. A few choice words bubbled to the surface. He suppressed the tornado of tyranny threatening to unleash from his mouth.

He strode over to the crashed book half covered in mud. It stuck to the sloping side of the canal by another aggressive weed. He bent over to examine it. The book glowed with a bioluminescent light. Spiderweb cracks formed along the binding. The heat it was emitting caused the water to bubble, steam rising in rapid mushroom bumps.

"Rozul! Look!" The radiation from the glowing cracks initiated an instant sunburn. He squinted and averted his gaze.

Rozul's plastic face melted into a frown. He pulled his straw hat down around his squiggly ears. "This doesn't bode well. Will it explode? Will we soon...well, now. I believe my language matrix is broken too. What does the 'kicking of a bucket' have to do with death? We will be unable to kick buckets when our atoms are splitting apart from the power of another universe."

The canal water near them bubbled into a frenzied jacuzzi cranked up high. Time slowed down. Ri didn't know what he should do. Watch the book explode? Grab it and risk a burn? Could he somehow retrieve it from the water without touching it? His wrestling thoughts piled on top of one another, losing and collapsing from defeat.

A loud splash startled him from his paralysis. Rozul jumped into the canal, the water flowing around his tall knee trees. "Jacuzzi. Ah, yes, I see. Quite nice. Great idea." He propelled his big hands through the dirty water with the innocence of a toddler wading through a kiddie pool.

Ri frowned. He hadn't mentioned the word "jacuzzi" aloud. Could Rozul read his mind? No time for minor concerns. "The boiling water doesn't hurt you! Quick, grab the book! It's overloaded or something."

Rozul, the obedient sidekick, sprang into action. He untangled the blood-hot book from the singed weed. He lifted it up, and the water crackled and sizzled into vapor. The cracks extended from the book and infected him. The golden bioluminescence spread from Rozul's gloves. It traveled along his stick arms and torso and up his cue ball.

Ri's lower jaw dropped, and he pointed at Rozul with his eyes wide open. "What's happening? Is that supposed to happen? Is that supposed to be happening to me?"

Rozul examined his body, an amused half-smile cracking up the rim of his mouth. "Ah. Yes. The memories."

"It doesn't hurt?"

"Well, some do. Such are the nature of memories."

"Hold on, Shadows. You're hogging all the memories. Tell me now, I need to know. What are you remembering?"

"What? Oh, nothing. These memories must be yours. You need to eat them first."

Ri jammed his palm into his hip. "What? Are you babbling baloney again?"

"Well, not yet. They aren't done. Cooked? Solidified? Solid? Human words, so inadequate. But these must be your memories and not mine, since I cannot eat them." Rozul jammed a white finger glove at his painted mouth.

The fractures along the book vanished—the thirty or so cracks covering Rozul's body also faded. The intense light and heat they emitted dissolved. Soon, only fat, brown slug-type creatures wriggled and thrashed in place.

Ri made a face. "Ugh, really? Leeches?" Although leeches weren't found where he lived, he had learned about them from classmates and Google. Leeches were gross. "Why did the memories become leeches?" He wasn't sure he actually wanted to know the answer.

"That's how you eat them."

"Disgusting."

Rozul turned to adjust his straw hat—presumably to find out why eating leeches was an Earth blunder—and lost his balance. He tripped over his long legs and big feet and fell backward into the water.

Ri waited to react. A big goofy wooden and plastic alien unscathed by boiling water shouldn't get hurt from a little fall.

When he spotted the real problem, he almost fell backward too. The leeches leaped away. They skimmed along the water's surface, surfing tadpoles sailing down the canal. He shouted, "The memories! They're getting away!"

Rozul's big clumsy body splashed around, hastening the leech exodus. He tripped over his origami-self again and crumpled. Ri jumped to attention and raced alongside the canal. The dirt slope covered with trash and weeds slowed him down, so he sprinted up the edge along the flat road. Some universal force propelled the leeches forward, and he fell behind fast. The leeches sped away and faded into the horizon, surfing in the direction of the wider canal a mile up the road.

No matter how fast he ran, he would never catch up. The dirty water camouflaged the small dark slugs. His memories gone. Forever.

Coming to a halt, he stared at his feet. The old familiar rage gripped him from head to toe, ringing through his ears. He clenched his fists, and his arms shook. His body flooded with hot adrenaline. He wanted nothing more than to punch something with repeated blows until he collapsed from exhaustion.

He lost track of how long he stood there, wrestling his own will and rebellious body. He seethed with red rage, and time dissolved. Awareness of his surroundings faded into a vast, endless sea.

From a distance, Rozul's annoyingly chipper voice pierced through his field of fury. "Ri. Ri. Ri! What do you see, Ri? Why did you come to a grinding salt?"

Ri limped around and lumbered back in retreat. He shuffled his heavy feet through the powder dirt. He listened to his hijacked sanity wind down into discernable thoughts.

Rozul sat on the dirt beside the canal, his long tree legs dangling and his feet resting in the dirty water. He held the book under his armpit. "You look...distraught? Disheveled. Disappointed? Am I close?"

"Cool it with the vocabulary words, okay?"

"What's wrong?"

Ri had no energy left to keep seething, although he did channel his inner devil. "Dude. Where've you been? We lost all the memories! Did you not notice them cruising down the canal? We lost our only clue! Now, how are we supposed to fix the broken moon, Shadows? I wanna give up! We gotta fix all the black hole heads. We gotta fix my mom!" He crossed his arms hard and plopped down next to Rozul. His legs dangled above the flowing water.

Rozul remained silent. He probably realized his wacky words of wisdom fixed nothing. Rozul handed the book to Ri. "We have this. It's something."

He took the book and fixated on it. What an unusual thing. What else remained hidden inside? Were the memories forever lost? Were there any other clues to discover? If the leeches were only his memories, could they still get Rozul's missing memories out?

Rozul flapped his plastic tongue. "Life is chock-full of obstacles. Expect them. Then the appearing obstacles will cause no disappointment."

Ri's churning mood boiled over and splashed against Rozul. "Shadow Man. You're clumsy. If you hadn't fallen over your ginormous self, we'd have tons of helpful memories. Nope. Nada. Nothing. That's no obstacle. That's you, failing hardcore. Own it."

He instantly regretted his words. Fortunately, Rozul possessed unpredictable alien reactions. Rozul lifted a forefinger high. Next, he adjusted his straw hat. "Ah. I see. Dimensional settings, off-kilter. Hmm, I concede your point. Definite oversight." He smirked.

Ri dropped his shoulders. The weight from the broken moon crushed his will. Was he even smart enough to save his precious mom? *Maybe I'm not. Maybe this is hopeless.* Something interrupted his dark thoughts and tickled his pinky finger. He scanned the book, ready to swat away a fly. A leech wriggled between the pages, struggling to escape, squirming with determined defiance.

His eyes popped open wide. "A memory!"

8

The Malevolent Memory

ROZUL CLAPPED HIS MONSTROUS mitts together, spraying brown water droplets on Ri. "What are you waiting for? Eat it!"

Ri gulped and wrinkled his nose. "Um. Are you sure there isn't another way? Should we cook it first? Microwave it or something?"

Rozul laughed, an ill-timed, unprecedented cosmic chortle. "Infrared and microwaves. Are you aiming to *destroy* the memories? Stop squandering time. You're the one in the big hurry. Eat it."

Ri despised displaying weakness. He snatched up the leech, dangled it above his mouth, and closed his eyes. He whispered to himself, "It's a hotdog. It's a hotdog. A wriggling, slimy, brown and bloody hotdog..."

He winced. Then he dropped it down his throat, waiting for what might happen to his stomach by ingesting them alive.

His taste buds exploded with dark chocolate and burnt marshmallows. "It's sweet! Not nasty at all!"

Rozul tilted his big cue ball. "Ah. A good memory. Excellent."

Then Ri's mind bent.

The memory exploded in his mind, and he was no longer sitting along the canal. He was riding on a skateboard. He cruised down a sidewalk with the cool wind whipping against his face. He savored bagels and cream cheese, the lingering aftertaste of breakfast. The neighborhood seemed unfamiliar, though it hinted at a comforting homeliness.

He glided effortlessly down the smooth pavement, powering the skateboard with strong kicks. His heartbeat drummed rhythmically inside his chest along with strong breaths. Inside the memory, he turned an abrupt right, skidding to a stop with effortless control. He jumped off the skateboard and popped it upright, grabbing the board with his left hand. He jogged down the alley behind a vaguely familiar maroon brick house. He approached a dumpster and strolled behind it.

Ri struggled to make sense of the living memory. He had a hard time adjusting his mind to the alien experience. He had expected to remember something to fill in his missing gaps. But no. This person's memories did not seem like Ri's. This mystery boy rode skateboards with skill and *liked* cream cheese. Ri tried to think his own thoughts while experiencing this memory, but his mind blended within the powerful flow. His own self melted away. He followed—an intruding observer—hoping that understanding the connection to this unknown boy would come later.

The boy in the memory remained calm at the same time Ri's observing self recoiled. A five-foot-tall rat stood on his hind legs. The rat donned a leather jacket and ripped jeans. Glowing copper eyes encircled by crusted platinum fur greeted him. The rat smiled and revealed razor-sharp metal teeth. The tip of the rat's nose shined, constructed of sleek metal. The rat's body stiffened and turned sideways. He revealed an intermingled mesh of muscle, fur, leather skin, and plates of metal. A phrase bubbled up inside Ri's consciousness—*intelligent rat-cyborg. Weird.*

The rat uttered a deep growl. "You came. A risk. Figured you'd smell the bait."

Ri's mind flowed into perfect rhythm with the mystery boy. The boy replied, "Quit wasting my time, Belez. Your breath reeks of last year's Cheez Whiz. I brought the money."

"Careful speaking my name, meatbag. Too much power for this 'verse. I put it under the dumpster. Wait until I leave, and five minutes later, retrieve it—not a second before. No one can track me. You? You leave behind a quantum trail with the stealth of a baby eating a cookie. Humans are filthy."

A voice inside Ri's mind, part of the boy's memory, muttered, *A rat calling me filthy, wow, so ironic.*

The boy reached inside his pants and pulled out an envelope stuffed with cash. He handed it over.

Belez stuck out his long tongue and wiped it across his metal teeth. "You sure this condensed tech has data?"

"Whatever. Check it. And stop calling me a liar."

The rat lifted the envelope toward the noon sun. "I sssseee it. The connections are clear." The rat pulled open his leather jacket and stuck the envelope in his breast pocket. "The next universe we do business in, patience is a luxury. It's gonna cost you much more to save all these worthless mammals. There ain't enough energy for everyone."

"You parrot a scarcity mindset. Those rules are misapplied everywhere. We fix the greed, and these mammals will produce their share. You'll see."

"Dreamer. Idealist. Dummy. Your misguided beliefs are unimportant, provided you keep the data flowing."

The boy-memory stuck out his thumb. "We done? Because your breath is worse than this dumpster."

The rat lifted his right paw and pointed a razor nail at the boy's chest. "You dare disrespect me? You might play entrepreneur, but 'chew don't got dah heat, sonny." Dozens upon dozens of regular earth rats emerged from the shadows. They crept forward and surrounded the boy, forming a calculated threat. Small, regular rodents. A shiny glint in their eyes revealed the rat-cyborg controlled them in a deadly way.

The boy shrugged.

The rat laughed, a sinister, controlling chuckle echoing from a deep, faraway place. "I respect you, kid. You've got spunk. You can overdo cocky, though. Not everyone appreciates your unorthodox ideas. There are powers in place nastier than me, who tolerate no threats. They see pathways before you even think of 'em. If you grow too full of yourself, they'll crash your little enterprise before its heart starts pumping."

"Thanks for the lecture."

The rat tilted his head sideways and drummed his claws across his chest.

The rat dissolved.

The boy leaned back against the dilapidated wooden fence near the dumpster. He kicked his foot up. He glanced at his watch after thirty seconds, shrugged, and dropped down. He focused on a small, plastic cobalt dome attached underneath the dumpster. The boy reached for it.

It exploded.

The memory leapfrogged out of Ri's mind.

He gasped and wheezed. Clutching his chest, he almost fell forward into the canal. Rozul steadied him with his giant glove, holding his legs with a firm grip.

"I don't understand!"

Rozul swirled his chin paint. "Hmm. That happens often with you."

"I thought we found *my* memories. I crawled inside, or listened, or somehow experienced another boy's memories."

"Interesting. Are you certain it wasn't *you* in the future?"

"No, listen! No way, not me. This boy can ride a skateboard and is super strong and tough and smart. And he wheeled illegal deals with alien rats. Cyborgs."

Rozul's painted expressions whirled. He tapped his hat, accessing his database of language, interpreting Ri's words.

Ri's upper lip twitched. "A rat. A stinkin' rat. A big, ugly rodent with gross teeth and disheveled fur. Humongous and taller than me. It could speak. Partly made of metal, with robot sections. Doesn't ring any alarm cow bells?"

"Is this big talking metal rat a normal occurrence here?"

"Not at all! His speech reminded me of a cross between an old person and a hipster who watched too many gangster movies. Strange."

"Yes, indeed."

"Oh, yeah, his name was Belez."

Rozul froze.

Not a good sign. Ri threw an emphatic wave. "Hey. Big dummy. You okay?"

Rozul rotated his oversized head in a slow and dramatic way. He whispered, "Are you *certain* about the name, Belez?"

"Ha! Yes! This memory burned deep inside my brain. I remember every detail. I still smell the hot nasty Cheez Whiz on the rat's breath. Let me tell you the entire memory, play by play."

Afterward, Rozul hardly reacted. Ri peppered him with questions. "Well, what's going on? I told you it's not my future memory, and not something happening in my past. Whose memory is it, then? Do you know this boy? Who is Belez?"

Rozul's entire body shook. "Shh! Stop articulating his name so loud. It has power in every universe."

Again, Ri fought the urge to kick something. "Ugh! These memories are supposed to give us answers, not pile up more questions. I thought it would help us fix the broken moon. Find a way to fix the adults. Get my mom her head back. I bet the other memories were stuffed with better clues." He lost his nerve when Rozul acted all shook up. "Shadows. Who is the bad rat? Why are you squirming the way Shelly Sanderson does after giving the wrong answer in class?"

A silver grape-sized tear formed at the bottom of Rozul's right eye. It hovered and shimmered in the light. It rolled down his plastic cheek and landed in the powder dirt with a soft splash. The emotional display sent Ri's arm hair shooting straight up.

He slapped Rozul on the back of his leg. "Um. Chin up. We've got more work to do, that's all. More clues to find. Crying over lost leeches never gets anyone anywhere. What did you say a moment ago? Expect bad things to happen? Well, evil rat-cyborg is bad. Now we figure out our next play." Ri shuffled over to his bike and backpack lying against the berm of the canal. Shoving the book into his overfilled backpack took some maneuvering.

Rozul's plastic face gazed upward, watching the clouds. "Okay. Please allow me to relate a story first and then you'll grasp why I've lost my...bones? Blood vessels? Nerve endings? Ah, haven't yet mastered your language. Anyway..."

A loud voice booming through a megaphone interrupted their conversation. "Rieden Reece! Move away from the canal and step toward me, now!"

A shiny silver limousine skidded to a stop haphazardly in the dirt. The odd vehicle sprayed flames and dust from its four shiny mirror tires. A tall figure wearing a silver suit with a black hole head shimmered in the sunlight. A secret agent alien, that's what they looked like. Somehow, Ri heard the adult voice speaking via megaphone. No time to analyze why.

"Rieden Reece!" the voice shouted again.

Time to run!

9

The Dump Dive

RI FLUNG ON HIS backpack, grabbed his bike, and jumped on. He pedaled with a mad fury down the dirt walkway along the canal. He raced toward the railroad tracks and jumped his bike off the dirt road into the alfalfa field.

The strange vehicle tried to follow along the dirt road. But Ri biked at full speed, moving away at a 45-degree angle while mowing down the alfalfa. The alfalfa grew to the perfect height, giving his tires great traction. The strange vehicle swerved into the southwest corner of the field and climbed up the rolling hill toward the railroad tracks. Ri crossed the tracks and landed in the desert wilderness. His tires struggled to move through the soft sand as he followed the railroad tracks on the south side. Rozul bounced along on his right side with zero sense of urgency.

The strange alien vehicle had no way to follow without four-wheel drive. The booming megaphone voice melted into the distance, but Ri didn't slow down—not yet. He kept his head low and pedaled with every ounce of his strength.

Ten minutes and two passing trains later, Ri detoured and cut across the wilderness. He dismounted his bike and walked it with care while wheezing in the heat. Rozul's oversized feet plodded through the desert sagebrush and crushed cacti. Ri attempted to scold him, though his words ripped out in spurts.

"Shadows. Watch out. Snakes, spiders, and scorpions. Quit stirring them up. They may not hurt your alien body, but they can bite or sting me. Doctors can't help me with their black hole heads."

Rozul's painted face peered down at the wilderness. "Ah, yes. Cactus. That would explain my sharp shooting pain. Smart plan to avoid the secret agent. Come out here to no man's la la land."

Ri steered his bike out of the way of a large sagebrush. He hoped the dozens of burrs stuck in his tires wouldn't pop his thorn-resistant tubes. Taking a deep breath, he tried to speak in a normal voice, though his heart still beat too hard. "Who was that secret agent? How did they know where to find us? Are they here because you busted the moon?"

"Me? No. The agent shouted *your* name."

"What? Why me? Did you see that crazy alien? Wearing some strange silver suit and flames flashing out of their vehicle? Not human. Unless... Do you think the agent works for the Librarian of Death?"

"It is not clear. More obstacles." Rozul swirled the paint on his chin like he was trying to solve an annoying math problem.

Ri wiped away sweat from his brow. "Sure. Yeah. Another problem to solve—who is this agent and why are they chasing me? We need to go somewhere and regroup. I've got a place in mind. It's the perfect hideout. Another half a mile and we'll reach the other side of town. Plus, I'm dying of thirst." The sweat between his shirt and backpack was rubbing his back raw.

"Yes. There we can formulate a clear plan of action. How to stitch your moon back together and fix the dark rip through your universe."

They walked in silence. Ri fumbled to organize his thoughts—replay his new memory and the escape from the agent. How he could use the new info to save his mom. But all he could think about was the heat and his thirst. His thoughts tunneled in on his discomfort.

When they arrived at Ri's target, Rozul grabbed the brim of his hat with both gloves. "On the list of top ten worst ideas ever within the infinity of universes, this, my little meat friend, takes all the dessert!"

Ri stared with abject silence and awelessness.

Rozul cleared his plastic throat. "Ahem. Sarcastic comedy? Supposed to elicit a chuckling response. Did I jumble up the order of words?"

Ri walked his bike behind the building. He nestled it between the dumpster and gunk-caked concrete steps. The zipper on his backpack jammed while he yanked out his precious book. He draped his backpack over the handlebars. "Dude. Please stick to breaking universes. Nobody learns comedy in a day. You're either funny or die of embarrassment."

Rozul gestured at the bar with both gloves shaped into finger guns. "Why are we entering an establishment serving intoxicating liquors? It's chock-full of emotionally stunted adults with too much disposable income. That they've no doubt earned at disappointing and dissatisfying places of employment."

"Bro! Did you switch search engines? Stick to Google. You sound more ridiculous than my grandma's old encyclopedia. It's the Sunshade Bar. I hear the bartender's cool. Great place to hide."

Rozul reached down and yanked wilderness debris from the bottom of his oversized feet. He bent his body, feet, and cue ball head in impossible directions. "Are you not wary of the adults with black hole heads?"

"What? No. So, I'm guessing wherever you come from, they don't have bars? Before my mom and dad divorced, my dad used to take me to bars all the time. Taught me how to shoot pool." Pulling up the memory caused his mind to skip tracks. Like trying to remember bits from a fading dream. Was that an aftereffect from eating the leech? Ri shook it off. "The point is that nobody cares what you do in a bar. Black hole heads or not, people mind their own business."

Rozul straightened up and continued to resist his idea. "You're too young to enter a bar."

"With an adult, I'm good. You pass for an adult. A goofy, plastic, and somewhat wooden-giraffe kind of adult."

Ri trudged around the building with Rozul lumbering behind. "You forget. I'm invisible to everyone else."

"Listen up. You've failed to tap into all your superpowers yet. You're wielding some heavy-duty-universe-molecular-smashing-off-the-charts-energy. Whip up a hologram or something techy to project a fabricated image."

Rozul folded his arms and tapped the skinny sides of his torso with his large gloves. "Your perception of reality here is disturbing."

Ri wrapped his fingers around the broken handle of the dilapidated wooden door. He gripped the book tucked under his right arm. He faced Rozul with a wry smile curling upward. Escaping from the agent had spiked his adrenaline. He licked the invincibility on his lips. "Yo, brother from another universe's mother, we got this. Now, shut up and let me do the talking. If you're invisible to them, they'll think I'm talking to myself. They gotta ignore me. I'm another delinquent kid doing delinquent things, capiche?"

Ri swung the door open wide. The odor from decaying cigarette smoke and dying germs assaulted his nose. He wrinkled it and stepped into the dingy establishment. It took a moment for him to adjust to the darkness. The dim light rays—bent in impossible directions—sucked into the adults' black hole heads. Torsos with tattooed hands holding cue sticks and cheap beer turned toward him. It required little effort to avoid harsh gazes from curious adults without eyes. He climbed up onto an empty bar stool at the counter, his fingertips brushing something gooey he hoped was old gum. He dropped the book across his lap. Rozul sat down beside him, his towering, lumbering body looming over the counter.

The bartender waltzed up to them. She pointed her thick, greasy finger. The black hole head did something unexpected. She also pointed at Rozul.

Rozul grinned—his stupid plastic head incongruous inside the dirty dungeon. The surreal image reminded Ri of the movie *Slasher Death VIII* he'd watched at his friend's house. Rozul whispered too loud, "Oh, Snapple! She can see me!"

Ri elbowed him in the ribcage. "Of course."

Rozul slammed his glove on the counter. "Order me a volcano."

Ri had never heard of a volcano drink and doubted Earth sold them. He loathed exposing his ignorance to adults, though. He lifted two fingers. "Two volcanos, please, with extra, um, lava."

The bartender threw a dirty rag over her shoulder and turned away.

Rozul exhibited too much enthusiasm. "This is fun!"

"Quiet! Keep it down," Ri muttered. "You're too loud. People can see and hear you now."

"How are you doing this?"

"I'm not doing it. You are."

Rozul scratched his straw hat. "Are you certain?"

Ri leaned across the counter. His short torso made the angle unnatural. He stretched and whispered, "Pay attention. I've been thinking. It's the memories. I've seen this before in movies. Those leeches we lost in the canal could've filled in all these missing blanks. Somehow, when you traveled to my universe and broke the moon, it caused pieces of this timeline to fall apart. Memories trapped in secret locations. You're capable of appearing human and so much more. You've tapped a small fraction of your powers, bro. You're a powerful Thor, or something, who's forgotten who you are."

Rozul stroked his swirling chin with a contemplative finger. "Interesting. It calculates." He lifted a stick arm and mimicked flexing a nonexistent muscle. "Thor is stronger, I presume."

"Ugh. Okay, yes, you're a pathetic weakling compared to Thor. You've got all this lightning power, you follow? Tapping into the universal cosmos stuff, you hearing me? There's probably a better comparison... I've got nothing. A strange kind of superhero-being-thing. Like, like..."

Rozul's darting ink-eyes revealed an internet search for superhero names. "I'm a cooler version of Anti-Molecular Man!"

"Never heard of him. You've got the wrong universe."

Ri glanced at the mirror behind the row of alcohol. The adults shooting pool stared with electrical black holes. Rozul's reflection glowed a bit. The human-self he portrayed appeared old. Old, old. Gandalf in his retirement years. A large, busy beard grew from Rozul's human reflection. He smacked Rozul's arm and whispered, "Look at you."

Rozul stroked his straw hat—his human reflection rubbed a bald head. Ri speculated that reflection was what the other patrons in the bar saw, too. Did they perceive each other's black hole heads? Or did they believe in a fake normal while he alone accessed the broken reality? These questions churned his stomach acid.

Two volcanoes slammed down on the counter. Either the bartender was angry, or the bubbling mugs arrived with massive weight. Whipping out her rag, she wiped away some molten lava dissolving the countertop. She formed the rag into a whip and killed a big fly landing on her old cash register. She snapped her fingers and rubbed them against her thumb, indicating payment.

Ri had forgotten about that part.

Usually, he carried cash with him, or sometimes brought the debit card his mom gave him for emergencies. Even if he had his debit card, no way he wanted his mom to find out about this. How would she react? Drinking two volcanoes with an annoying alien at the diviest and dumpiest bar in Desert Lime, California, might be hard to explain.

Rozul banged Ri's stool too hard with his oversized feet. Rozul tipped his hat toward the book. Ri slanted the book sideways with his left hand and discovered something sticking out of the pages. Pulling it free took some effort—some magnetic force held it tight. He flipped the hunk of small paper around and recognized the familiar form. His mom's outdated checkbook.

Huh? How did that get here? It must have jammed into the book when he stuffed it into his backpack. But why was his mom's old checkbook that she never used anymore in his backpack? Ri struggled to connect the dots, but the memory remained hidden, behind a fuzzy wall. What a strange coincidence—the one thing he needed, the book provided. Did the book have a mind of its own—something more powerful than a simple memory container?

Ri shook away his questions and anxiety to focus on his current problem. Did people still even accept checks for payment? This ancient, dilapidated death dungeon might make an exception. He forced a fake grin for the impatient bartender.

He ripped out a blank check with his mother's preprinted address in the top left corner. It would take a couple days for her to notice the check, and by then he would've saved the universe. *Don't get mad, Mom. This is for you.* "I don't have a pen."

The bartender smacked the counter with her dirty towel. She tossed the towel back over her shoulder. She clutched the bubbling drinks with her bare hands and pulled them away.

Rozul shook his glove. "Wait." He tilted up his straw hat and removed a sleek, metallic pen with a gold tip. "Here, I forgot about this."

Ri snatched up the pen. He scribbled some numbers and a signature and waved the check at the bartender. The bartender lifted the check up to the dim light streaming in through the door crack. She clacked away on the register and threw the check inside, signaling with a thumbs-up. She sauntered away, using her towel whip to snap flies and an old sleepy guy at the other end of the bar.

Ri stretched his greedy grip and wrapped his hands around the volcano drink. The hot lava oozed down the side. The slimy goop tingled his fingers. The texture of it suggested toothpaste mixed with caramel syrup. They bumped their bubbling mugs together. He dipped his lips into the rainbow colors and exploding bubbles. Fireball candy flavor mixed with peanut butter chocolate tingled his tongue.

"This is awesome!"

"Told you, earthling. I know a thing or two concerning bars. I fail to recall how old I am. Doubtless it's older than humanity."

"What do we drink to?" Gold, lavender, and bronze suds dripped down his chin. He wiped the suds away with his short sleeve—it singed the cotton.

Rozul hoisted his volcano drink high. "How about to my dead sister?"

Ri almost dropped his drink. "What?!"

Rozul slammed his glass down—a large metallic tear dangled from a long eyelash. "Boy, do I have a terrible tale for you."

10

The Terrible Tale

A TWISTED-UP FIST OF glass shards punched the inside of Ri's gut. He remembered the feeling. It happened whenever his mother said, "There's something important to tell you...tonight," and he had to endure the torture all day waiting to hear the bad news.

He itched to rush the alien but compelled his big mouth to stay shut during Rozul's telling of his terrible tale.

Rozul removed his straw hat and rested it next to his drink on the bar. Without his hat, he appeared smaller and frailer. No longer a dangerous alien invading from another universe. Now he resembled a sad, unemployed clown. "Well. That's a deep subject. Are you familiar with Quantum Entanglement?"

The tips of Ri's cheeks burned. Not knowing answers to adult questions made him want to argue and throw punches. He trusted Rozul. Although he was a cumbersome and annoying alien, he never acted judgmental. "Er. Um. It's mentioned in some of my sci-fi books. It's too hard to explain."

Rozul's faraway wet-ink facial expression hardened. "Oh, yes. I forgot what universe I inhabited. Let's see...." He peppered his straw hat with movements made across a computer keyboard. His fat glove fingers danced with dizzying speed. "Oh. Interesting. You humans are born into this world quite messy. Okay, you grow inside a bag of fluid. The bag explodes, and the baby claws its way out while its mother screams with agony..."

"Gross! Shut up, man, I'm trying to drink my volcano. Yeah, I saw the birthing baby videos in health class. We can skip that lesson."

Rozul shoved his hat away and shivered. "Er, yeah. That's why you humans are so violent, it's kind of the first thing you do. Well, in my universe—the older and wiser one—we are born from star energy. A direct creation of quantum intelligence harnessed and molded by superior beings. Wise beings in existence for billions of your Earth years. Once in a dark matter demise—I'm talking every million or so years—something amazing happens. One of the manifestations-of-will loves his progeny so much, he decides to duplicate it. The process requires an entire solar system of energy. The result is a reflection, almost a copy—an equality. Quantum Entanglement."

Although Ri had consumed half his volcano, the lava bubbled and burned bright. The flavors shifted while he sipped the various layers. This layer slid down butter pecan crusted with burnt marshmallows. "Dude. You're trying to tell a terrible tale. I'm so lost right now. You're a star?"

Rozul blinked away his faraway fixation again. "Ah. My apologies. Memories. Such sweet and dangerous things. Here." He slid his straw hat closer to them, placing it between the two drinks. He flipped it over and waved his glove. A three-dimensional display appeared, followed by a shifting pattern of mesmerizing flowing colors. The manifested image represented the star theory he proposed. After a moment, the conglomeration of energy balls merged into a familiar shape: an outline of two human babies held in the arms of a loving mother.

Ri slammed his heavy mug down. "Ah! Twin babies. You're telling me about your twin sister."

Rozul paused, accessed his mental Google, and dropped a nod. "Yes. Closest equal on this planet. Twin sister. Except, our kind exists without distinct male and female design. You humans operate with a different set of chemical directives. More akin to a sister in the reflection of my less analytical side. Empath. That's the right word, empathy."

"Empathy-schmempathy."

"Excuse me?"

"Ignore me, continue. Twin sister."

Most of the details of Rozul's sister's life and experiences exceeded Ri's comprehension. When Rozul reached the end of his story, though, Ri conceived a somewhat vague interpretation.

"...she struggled to save me from the evil taking over our pocket of the cosmos. I told her not to. She meant everything to me. She understood my buried and unconscious thoughts. She would finish my sentences. She would hold my taxed and overused faculties. I never imagined or foresaw any part of my life without her. The equation always included her. Always."

A golden tear, a bead of shimmering liquid, squeezed from Rozul's eye and rolled down his cue ball cheek. It dangled for a split second and fell—defying gravity, softly spinning. The hovering droplet never touched the ground. It faded and disappeared.

Rozul cleared his throat. "Yes. Excuse me. So many fond memories are flooding back. She faced the evil alone, to protect me and our great family. She died. And not in the way you can rebuild. Her atoms disappeared, taking the evil with her."

Ri's tummy rebelled against the combination of sad story and volcano drink. "What do you mean, disappeared? Did she die or get childnapped?"

Rozul corrected him. "Kidnapped? No, not stolen. Lost. Disappeared. Missing. Her atoms jumped—our tracking system lost her. She misdirected the evil, taking on the brunt of its power alone. Our family's theory is she built a random path through an alternate, yet dormant, system to confuse the evil. Luring it into a, no, not a bear trap. A prison? Yes, no, not something similar here."

Ri rubbed Rozul's elbow. "I get it, giant shadow. She's trapped and missing. There's no way to rescue her?"

"Rescue?"

"Yeah. Go find where her atoms went. Locate, um, what'd you call it, the dormant universe or whatever."

Rozul patted his squiggly line ear as if forcing out trapped water. "Rescue. She's gone. Did you misinterpret my translation? It appears my filter system is out of whack-a-mole."

"No. Dude. I got it. You forgot to tell me the part making it impossible to find her. To figure out where she dragged the evil. Save the day, devise a plan, collect your posse and track her location down. Rescue her from the evil, kill it with an anti-matter gun or something, and snag your sister back."

"She's dead. She's gone. She's ancient history channel."

A tremble in Rozul's voice made Ri's face flush. Rozul trembled in the similar way his mother did when she refused to hear the truth.

Ri pushed his half-finished drink away and leaned in, crowding Rozul's space. He tugged at Rozul's skinny arm. "Shadows. Listen! Wow, this drink makes my brain work in bizarre ways. Think about it. *That's* why you came to my universe. That's why everything fell apart here. *You* didn't break my universe. Your sister did! She brought the evil into my solar system. You're missing memories...you've forgotten. *That's* why you're here. Listen. It all makes sense, now. You searched for your sister and followed the path to her. The evil figured it out and set a trap for you, or your sister blocked her path or something. Yes, yes, yes. This isn't about me fixing the moon and the broken adults. It's about finding your sister and killing the evil!"

Rozul shook his head back and forth in slow motion. It took him a moment to respond. "Okay. So, you're saying my sister is still alive. She broke the moon. And I followed her here. So, if we find her, then the two of us, with our power combined, can stitch the moon back together. We can pull all the released energy back into place and realign the structure on an atomic level. It will fix the dark rip through your universe and all the adults will get their heads back."

Ri shouted, "Yes! Yes! Yes! And my mom will go back to normal!"

"But what about our missing memories? And what about the Librarian of Death and the mysterious universal agent who are tracking us?"

"Listen. Shadows." Ri's voice echoed through the bar. "We've got it now! I see the plan clear as day. We've had it out of order. We have the book. But we need to find your sister too. She's the most important piece of this whacked-out puzzle. And the Librarian of Death and the universal agent? Pshaw. Lame-O's. We can avoid those losers all day long. We're unstoppable!"

Ri burped and stopped shouting. All the bodies beneath the black hole heads rotated. An adult holding a cue stick rhythmically beat the stick into his palm.

Shrinking into the barstool, Ri spied on the adults via the mirror. Even the bartender stood there, her hands on her hips. Something new captured everyone's attention. A beam of light reflected from the mirror. He whipped around. The same silver secret agent from the canal stood at the threshold. One silver-gloved hand gripped its hip; the other held a large laser cannon on its shoulder.

Ri and Rozul shouted simultaneously, "Run!"

Rozul's large body bounded and bounced to the back of the bar. Ri dodged through aggressive adults grabbing and reaching to snatch him. He flung the book at Rozul so he could maneuver better. One adult reached and clutched his bicep. Ri twisted too quickly and slid down across the floor. He crawled between a barstool and the counter, knocking against the old man's cowboy boot. His escape lacked grace—he managed to slip away. He ran straight into the bathroom, ripped open the slider window, and crawled through it. He crashed into the hot dirt.

Sunlight! *Time to go!* An emergency siren drowned out the beating of his heart.

11

The Annoying Assistance

ROZUL JOGGED WITH LIGHT, lumbering steps, while Ri hammered at his bike pedals. Rozul pondered aloud in his nonchalant way, "Explain to me again why we're risking attending your school. Won't you discover double trouble there?"

Ri's breathing leveled off. Pedaling fast made talking difficult. "Stuff. In my locker. Cash. Snacks. My science kit. Plus, Brian Bowman. Give help."

"Brian? Isn't he the child you poke fun at each day? Why do you require help from a...'goober-head'? Do you believe we can trust him?"

"Don't. Be. Jealous. Smart. Help with book. Now, shut up."

Ri's stomach flipped somersaults. Hunger, the volcano drink, the adventure, and the anticipation of solving the puzzle. Those things amplified his erratic emotions. He hyper-focused his attention. He needed to sneak to his locker. Talk to Brian. Retrieve more memories. Fix the universe.

Fix his mom.

He slowed down upon approaching the school. The sky changed colors. Moondust shards sliced through the sky. They resembled bits of pointed glass falling from a steady rain. The moon shards shimmered and sparkled, ripping up reality with the finesse of flaming fiberglass. A piece of moondust sliced at his arm. He threw Rozul an adrenaline-filled look of contempt. Rozul's painted face dissolved into a grimace.

Ri approached the school grounds from the far south side with caution. He hid his bike next to the usual pile of old collected trash and snuck under the bent section of the wire fence. The sun peeked past the ominous sky. A group of teachers congregated at the north end of the school complex. Lunchtime. The teachers often neglected to monitor the locker area.

He serpentined the mob of kids meandering in different directions. Some students messed with their lockers. Some rushed toward the lunchroom. Some headed to the bathrooms. Others stood in groups talking. No one paid attention. He preferred loner life. He despised their idiotic cliques.

He stepped around the concrete benches and approached his locker. He seized the dial to spin his combo, only to yank his fingers away. Fire ants. Every. Single. Day. No matter how many times Ri killed those stupid ants, they came back. The ants had plagued him for the entire school year. Oh no, his food...

Ri brushed away the dozen or so ants marching up his locker hinge. He spun the combo, whipped open the door, and found his bag of sour gummy poppers destroyed. The ants were devouring them, hundreds sliming up his sugar stash. His stomach growled louder than he did. Rozul peered over Ri's shoulder, pressing into his personal space. Rozul gazed into the locker like it might contain a portal to his home universe.

"Dude. You're crowding. Can the other kids see you?"

"No. That trick only worked in the bar. Dunno how you fabricated that scheme."

Ri yanked the compromised candy from his locker and flung it into the nearby trash can. He brushed away the stinging ants and ignored two annoying girls pointing and giggling at him. He returned to his open locker, dug out the hidden cash, and stashed it in his front pocket. He rifled through the locker's contents to retrieve his science kit. His blood pressure kicked up a notch until a latent memory surfaced. The kit lay buried inside his bedroom closet.

A hand reached over the top of his locker and waved the door in his face. Ri exhibited negative zero patience. He slammed the door shut so hard the metal clanging reverberated down into the concrete. "Seriously, Shelly, you gotta stop..."

Brian Bowman stood there, clutching his stack of books, chortling. His laugh erupted in a half snort, half growl. He nudged his Star Wars glasses up the bridge of his nose and cracked an awkward smirk. "Tsk, tsk. Trouble in paradise? You and Shelly fighting, eh? The dark side of her dating a degenerate."

Every word Brian spoke dug into his skin. He controlled it since he required Brian's brain. He grabbed Brian's collar with an irrefutable grip. "Come on, dufus. You gotta check something out for me."

Brian pushed him away. "I said stop calling me that."

Ri shrugged. "Fine. Whatever. Genius. Put your magic mind to good use. Let's go to the gym."

Brian spun the combo on his own locker. Ri refused to wait. He forced his way into the crowd of gossiping kids. Brian would follow. He had inherited Asperger's or Autism or something similar. They weren't supposed to mention it—the teachers labeled it bullying. Ri wasted zero time on matters not affecting him. All he knew for certain—Brian's nerdy personality annoyed everyone. Although his classmates put up with him, Brian had no real friends. Brian annoyed Ri, but so did all the other kids. Ri lived in a constant state of annoyance. Putting up with Brian proved no additional challenge.

Truthfully, he doubted Brian had any "A" disorder labels. Brian simply lacked self-control and vomited his nerdiness everywhere.

Ri waited by the basketball hoop and leaned on the pole, kicking one foot up. Rozul hung from the net swinging and waved his straw hat around, cowboy style. His behavior resembled a five-year-old, not a five-million-year-old.

Brian erupted through the gymnasium door with the discretion of a hurricane. He half jogged and half waddled across the basketball court. Brian reached him and halted, pushing up his glasses to focus his intense scrutiny. "It's dark in here. We're not allowed here. You heard the teachers are looking for you. And not for ditching. Mr. Coldbell talked to an officer in the principal's office. Someone said it's because you assaulted Shelly."

Oh. And never tell Brian a secret. No amount of money in the world could pay Brian to keep his big fat mouth shut.

Ri groaned. "I didn't hurt Shelly." At least, he didn't *think* he had hurt Shelly. Had he accidentally scratched her instead of scraping cotton candy from her face? The broken Earth twisted up the facts and skewed reality. He sucked down a deep breath. "I need your help."

Brian snorted and mimicked a high-pitched voice. "Am I your only hope? Hee hee!"

Ri ignored Brian. "This book. Find a way to extract information. Find memories. Or clues. Or something else important." He pulled it from his backpack and gently handed it to Brian.

Brian read the title aloud, "*Emergency Preparation for Disasters.* What? You preparing for a zombie apocalypse? Or writing a report?"

Ri seized the book from Brian's feeble grip and held it up to the dull light crawling through the sky windows. Still black. Still blank. He flipped through chunks of bone-dry pages. He shook the book at Brian. "This looks like a normal library book to you?"

"Eh. By normal you mean what? It's boring. Is there something special I'm missing?"

He handed the book back to Brian. "Geeker. Focus. Look at it. Does something pop out at you? Use your supersized brain. Think. Analyze. Decipher."

Ri cracked his knuckles while waiting for Brian's brain to kick into gear. Brian tucked the book beneath his arm. He removed his glasses and wiped the lenses with the bottom of his R2-D2 t-shirt. He replaced his glasses and sat down on the gym floor with the book open wide. Brian turned one page at a time.

Rozul hopped down from the net and scrutinized Brian, holding his chin with his white glove. "You think this boy will dig down answers?"

Ri shrugged. "Dunno. Worth a shot."

Brian looked up. "What?"

Ri slapped on an insincere grin. "Worth a lot. To you. If you find the answer."

Brian dipped his head and resumed reading. He coughed and chortled, "This is cool. Ants can consume a dead human's body, bone and all, in the desert in one week. Gone. Poof."

Ri's face burned hot. The overreaction ignited, and he failed to cool down the furnace blazing inside. He reached down where Brian sat cross-legged and ripped the book from his grip. "Come on, Rozul, we gotta escape this prison. Nothing here the inmates can help us with." Why had he been so foolish to think Brian might be able to help? Ri would have to figure everything out on his own, as per usual.

"Wait, where are you going?" said Brian.

While storming toward the exit, Ri shoved the book into his backpack.
He ignored Brian's high-pitched protests.

Rozul bounced along behind in complete obedience.

12

The Big Bully

B RIAN CHASED AFTER R I all the way back to his locker. His
classmates had deserted the locker area; most of them were busy
devouring their lunch. He would be more exposed if a teacher roamed
by. He needed to hurry up and get out of here.

Brian cried out, "Man, oh man, I'm sorry. I'm totally lost..."

Ri whipped around and pointed his finger. "Keep it down! It's over.
You've got no access to what's at stake here. Let me ask you one question:
have you noticed anything funny regarding adults' heads?"

Brian narrowed his eyes. "Adult heads? No. Why? What?"

Ri exchanged glances with Rozul. Rozul offered, "Is he lying due to
fear?"

Ri stifled his laughing out loud at Rozul's lame suggestion. No way
was Brian lying. Brian had the worst lying skills ever. If Brian had seen
the adult black hole heads, he would've bellowed that announcement to
the entire school. No. Brian was an open book, easy to read. He hadn't
seen anything.

Reopening his locker, Ri fished around the disarray. He clutched an
old, mangled granola bar. Someone shoved the door of the locker against
his arm. He shouted, "Brian!"

Not Brian. Ian Ice. His real last name was Hice, though the nickname
fit nice. He was by far the worst bully in seventh grade. Unfortunately

for their school, more bullies attended there than the average amount. A slew of fresh teachers would begin each school year. The new recruits trembled at the never-ending wave of bullies. The hierarchy of bullies avoided bothering Ri. He managed to stay off their radar most of the time.

Yet, something caught Ian Ice's attention. "Look who's here. Ditching class. Or not? Can't make up your own mind? Lost without your protector? I hear you're getting arrested."

Ri plucked his arm from the locker and Ian's grip. Ian stood only a couple inches taller. Ian spent all his free time wrestling, running track, and lifting weights. Ri would never beat Ian in a fist fight nor outrun him. His temper was already spiraling out of control, so maybe a good hard knock in the skull from Ian's fist would do the trick to cool him off. He self-observed his self-destructive thoughts...nothing could stop them. His starving exhaustion mixed with stress consumed him. Not a great combo for dealing with a bully.

Ian pushed his index finger into Ri's ribcage. "Hello. You listening, dreamer? You think you can handle juvie? I've been told what they do to the smart-mouth kids."

Brian stood to Ian's right, his jaw open and staring. Another kid, one of Ian's henchmen, stood to the left. Rozul—invisible and twice their height—towered over them from behind. His painted eyes spread wide. Somehow, he found a bucket of popcorn and munched away with loud plastic crunching.

A bubbling cauldron of snarky retorts simmered inside Ri. He really, really, really wanted to shower Ian with his waterfall of insults. *Stop, Ri, stop.* He remembered his mother. The broken moon. The book. All the adults' heads. Landing in the principal's office for fighting would help nobody. The teachers ran scared of the bully's parents. They would hold him in detention all day and lie to his mother, distorting the facts.

Nobody had time for that.

"Look. Ian. I'm sorry..."

Ian's demeanor dripped arrogance, and he scrunched up his tough-guy face. Ian grabbed Ri's collar. "No, you listen to me. I heard what you did to Shelly. That's not cool. You don't mess with girls, no matter what."

Ri gulped down his confusion. Since when did Shelly show up on Ian's radar? Ri never paid attention to school politics. Did Ian have a crush on Shelly? Or Shelly's friend? Or had Shelly gotten mad and told Ian, and now Ian was playing the class cop? Regardless of Ian's motivations, Ri wouldn't escape without a fight.

"Sorry, man. I didn't mean to hurt Shelly..."

Ian squeezed Ri's shirt tighter and threw him up against the lockers, pinning his back against them. Rozul waved his big hands, vying for Ri's attention. He had zero-point-zero time for Rozul's antics.

Ian gritted his teeth. "You're a little punk. A pathetic know-it-all who's always acting above other people. I dislike you. Your attitude makes me wanna puke. I'm giving you two choices. I teach you a lesson after school down at the dirt lot. In front of Shelly. Or you apologize to Shelly, and I'll beat you down behind the old post office. This is between me and you."

Ian's bony knuckles jammed hard against Ri's collarbone, cutting off some of his oxygen and choking him. Ian pulled back and pushed harder, banging Ri's head against the lockers. His body shook and his limbs filled with fire. His natural instincts shouted at him to stay silent—but an unstoppable force of will seized him. "Not much of a choice, if you ask me. Either way, I get a beatdown, so why bother telling Shelly I'm sorry?"

Ian guffawed, let go of Ri's shirt, and palmed his head. The back of his head banged against the metal hinge of the lockers. Hairs ripped off and his scalp grinded into the metal.

"So, that's what you think, punk?" Ian spat. "You think mouthing off to me is gonna give you a better choice? I'm so done with you, split-brain. You're outta control, and I guess I'll teach you your lesson right here. Jimmy! Be my lookout. Rieden Reece is gonna drink his own blood."

Ri saw red. He lost access to his prediction abilities. There existed a fifty-fifty chance he would fight. He waited for Ian to throw the first blow. Ian pulled back his fist, and it flew forward with a sharp curve. Time slowed down to a snail's pace; he watched Ian's fist clench harder and create a wide arc. Time continued to slow. And slow. And slooowwww.

So...slow...time...crawling....

Ri blinked. How could he find time to blink? The flying fist hovered in place, aiming for him. Why was everyone frozen in place? The size of Ian's fist tripled. Correction: his view of the scene changed. Ian's body grew bigger. The lockers grew bigger. The circle of kids standing around the concrete benches grew bigger.

Rozul grew into a giant!

He connected the dwindling dots. He was shrinking. And shrinking. The air tasted different. The sunlight bent into psychedelic colors, and average sounds erupted into a roar. He shrank so fast that Ian's enormous fist flew in a wide arc above him, missing his face completely. The shrinking accelerated.

His perception failed to catch up with reality. He locked sights with a horrific creature. An alien dog with beady eyes and grotesque tentacles. The rational part of his brain refused to believe what he was seeing at first, but soon he couldn't deny it.

He was staring deep into the eyes of an ant.

And this specific ant tried to pick him up. Ri staggered backward, gravity playing tricks with his legs. He moved too fast, and his body twisted in wrong directions. He whipped around in a mad hurry. Instant mistake. A dozen Great Dane-sized ants stampeded toward him with clicking interest. Rozul's voice spoke within his mind:

"Climb on an ant. I will help you control it."

Ri hesitated. Everything was happening too fast, and he needed time to think. But there was no time. He would have to accept these annoying enormous ants as his only escape. His body froze in place, unwilling to touch their intimidating insect armor. He grimaced and forced a telepathic reply:

"Which one? And why..."

"The fifth one back in the corner. It has wings and can fly."

His heart hammered with the power of a runaway locomotive. His body surged with a new level of energy and speed. He focused on Rozul's request, ignoring the acid churning and burning his throat.

"There, there, nice ant. Excuse me, please...."

The ants flicked their feelers around, and rough leather rubbed his skin. They acted intent on helping. He shoved through the herd and found the ant with wings. The ant spread its wings wide, and he struggled to crawl on top of it.

Once he succeeded in wrapping his legs and body around the ant, he gripped the rough exoskeleton and waited, bracing himself.

The ant launched into flight, and Ri held on for dear life.

13

The Valuable Vantage

R I RECOVERED FROM THE astonishment of miniaturization. Slowly, he began to relax—at least as much as he could while flying on the back of an ant. Steering the ant through oversized air molecules required practice. He almost melted from Ian's nasty breath blasting out his virus-filled saliva. A confused and angry Ian shrieked orders at his little henchman, Jimmy Juliano. Ri had zero percent interest in sticking around to see what Ian would do. He pushed his body forward and guided the obedient ant. From his tiny vantage point, he soared on a supercharged jet.

A miniature Rozul cruised up alongside him on another flying ant. Rozul's plastic face appeared a little less lost. His painted pupils displayed a new, determined intensity. The wind whipped Ri's hair into a mad frenzy. "This is awesome! I knew you had some serious star power to let loose, Shadows. You shrank us in the nick of time. I can't wait to see what you do next."

Rozul slammed his white glove against his hat to keep it from blowing away. "Next? I need to master this ride first before I try anything new."

Ri grinned, the adrenaline rush pumping pure joy through his veins. "At least I won't get bugs in my teeth." He lifted his right fist into the air and practiced holding on to the ant with one hand.

Rozul's painted eyebrows dripped from the Google translate ticking away within his alien brain. "Oh, no, I guess not..."

Although he had never flown on ants before, Ri was experiencing something like déjà vu. Something felt so familiar about hanging with Rozul. Their snarky banter. A missing connection tugged at him from the back of his mind. The uneasy feeling of these missing memories caused him to claw at reality. Never mind. Now was not the time to stir up his anxiety. He lifted his head a little higher and breathed in the fast-moving air. He could no longer see the school. "How far can our flying ants travel before tiring?"

"Not forever. Where are we going?"

"What do you mean? This was *your* plan!"

Rozul slapped his glove against his hat before it flew away. "I'm only now getting the hang of my powers. My memories are full of gaps. This isn't too hard, though. Controlling space, intelligence, and size. Should we land and make a plan?"

Ri wished the glorious soaring sensation would last forever. He'd always dreamed of being a pilot. This cinched it for him. Nothing in the world could be better than being above and on top with complete control.

The flying ant dove into an evasive maneuver. The ant rotated sideways and almost dropped him. He grasped the coarse exoskeleton and scratched up his arms. "Whoa! What happened?"

Rozul pointed behind them. "There!"

Something bright and shiny with a rough diamond appearance. It hovered, locked into a mad orbit, a spinning top wobbling. Ri identified it immediately, his eyes lighting up. "Moon shard."

"There's a bunch coming our way," said Rozul.

They dove into a falling cloud of dense moon shards, much bigger than the ants. The rough diamond-shaped moon debris ripped through wind pockets, slicing and dicing spacetime. Vibrating sky rips reached for them with the intense power of other universes. The rips reached out to pull them through to the chaos from alternate space.

Ri hyper-focused. Time slowed down. He dodged the falling shards and avoided the ripped portals into other dimensions. He spun upside down, dove into impossible spins, and forced the ant to turn at almost ninety degrees. He spotted a second of free time within a gap between moon shards. "Rozul! It's time to stop flying! Our ants are too tired and we're gonna crash."

Rozul croaked through his trembling plastic frown, "What should I do?"

"Let's head straight down. A few seconds before landing, enlarge us. Not too fast or too hard, or else we'll break our necks from the fall."

Rozul raised his left glove to agree. A moon shard sliced across the palm of his glove and ricocheted against his straw hat. The hat blew away and disappeared. He cradled his hurt hand while dodging another onslaught of falling shards. Another shower of rock blades forced Ri's attention away as he swerved to avoid them; he lost sight of Rozul.

Steering the ant, Ri dove toward the ground. "Get us out of here!" he shouted, even though he doubted the ant could understand him.

He flew at a forty-five-degree angle, pushing the ant's speed to full velocity. The ant pulled its wings back and dove into freefall. The shard obstacles slammed across his path. He guided the ant effortlessly, dodging the sharp edges with laser-focused accuracy. The buildings loomed larger, the casting shadows shifted, and the shards dissipated.

Ri gritted his teeth. "Almost...there..."

He approached the ground too fast. He yanked his ant up to avoid crash-landing. The grass blades and flower petals stretched before him—daggers of death. He maneuvered the ant into cruising speed, waiting for Rozul to join so they could find a safe, level lot to land on.

The wind shifted. Rozul's ant flew erratically, in an enlarged oval twisting pattern. Ri hauled his ant up, his knuckles aching from holding on with life-or-death intensity. He flew up higher and higher. Dodging at breakneck speed, he avoided the sparse spattering of shards. He intercepted Rozul the moment a triple-sized shard slammed into his cue ball head. Rozul tumbled off his ant, and gravity tore him into a wild spin.

"Catch him!" Ri yelled at Rozul's rogue ant. The ant just kept on flying straight ahead, oblivious. *Useless.*

With no other option, Ri accelerated his own ant faster and harder than before. He calculated the trajectory of the angle, aiming to catch a fly cue ball. Except Rozul's body was flopping through the wind, his long limbs flailing.

Ri pushed harder and dove down, down, down. He caught up with Rozul's falling body. They inched closer and closer to the jagged and hazardous overgrown field. Rozul's flapping gloves came closer and closer. Ri reached out to grab hold of one. Too hard to grip. Too large. He leaned over farther. He snatched Rozul's wrist on another turn of his thrashing body.

A moon shard slammed across his path. He pulled too hard; he slipped off the ant and plummeted. Clutching the unconscious alien around the torso, he screamed, "Wake up! Enlarge us before we hit the ground!"

Rozul's painted eyes fluttered.

"Now! Now! Now!"

Ri held on to him with a death grip. Both of their bodies spun into an uncontrolled freefall. The grass blades glinted; sharp daggers planted and poised to cut them to pieces. His burning intellect failed to slow time to focus on how to stop the incoming dicey death.

"We're gonna die!"

Rozul's eyelids flipped open wide, two broken blinds flapping. The end arrived; Ri slammed his eyes shut.

A hundred baseball bats smashed into his back. He crashed and a heavy weight crushed his torso. No daggers cut his skin. Rocks jabbed into his spine—he cried out.

Adjusting to the bright sunlight took a moment. The air tasted normal, and the background sounds returned. Ri stretched out and clutched a clump of grass.

Normal size!

He surveyed his surroundings. A wooden fence. A couple of citrus trees. A doghouse. Some old piles of dog poop. He checked his legs and arms. Nothing broken or bleeding. His body ached.

He turned to his left and almost laughed out loud. Rozul's big head lay stuck inside a dog dish, and his skinny body bent toward the sky, his butt sticking straight up. "Klutz! Are you okay?"

He ripped the dish off his cue ball head. "Hmm. Rough landing."

"That's an understatement."

"Where are we?"

"Well, I hope we haven't slipped out of our universe. I can see now why you broke the moon coming here. Um, I'm guessing we're in someone's backyard. I sure hope their dog is friendly. By the size of that bowl, I'm guessing no."

Ri forced himself up off the ground with a slight wobble. Every bone and muscle in his body creaked. How far were they from the school? Had they landed in town? His surroundings whispered familiarity. He wiped away dead grass and dirt from his clothes. "Come on. Let's beat it before I get in even more trouble."

Rozul pulled his body upright, a dangling display of disjointed body parts. Ri studied the curious creature, a tad worried and a bit envious of his amazing abilities. If they could somehow harness his unpredictable power...

"Wait!"

Too late. Rozul stepped hard into a huge pile of dog poo. It smooshed all over his large feet.

Ri smacked his forehead. "Come on, ya big goober." He trudged around the house near the perimeter fence. His soft steps treaded the narrow walkway. Whose property were they trespassing on?

He couldn't resist sneaking a peek. He pressed his face against the living room side window and peered inside. Shelly Sanderson's cotton candy cheeks shined bright pink as she looked up at him. She screamed like a banshee.

Ri fell back against the fence and detected a loud dog snarling. He leaped and scrambled into full speed, screaming, "Run, Rozul, run!"

14

The Temper Tantrum

R I KICKED HARD AT the dirt. He stomped through an unfamiliar alley, unable to quiet his mom's voice lecturing him in his head: *"Don't do that to your shoes. You're going to ruin them."*

"Shut up!"

Rozul responded from behind. "What?"

"Wasn't talking to you."

"Oh. Is there someone else here?"

Ri groaned. "Why are you always so literal? I was talking to myself, out loud."

"You seem angry."

"You think?"

"Why are you angry?"

He spun on his heel to face the lumbering alien. "Oh. Yes. Brilliant question. Let's stop and think for a second. Um, let's see. We lost the book. I left my backpack and bike at school. You lost your straw hat, who knows what that means. It might mean all your powers or nothing. We almost died. We're nowhere closer to fixing my universe. We've lost memories with zero clues about what we're doing, why we're doing it, or what to do next. We haven't even found *time* to talk about the fact you came here to find your missing sister, which has *nothing* to do with me. For all you can remember, you randomly bumped into me after you cracked the moon and *thought* you should help me. Do you want me to go on? Because I can. I can keep going—there's a million more things I can list involving how bad we are failing at saving my world!"

Rozul crossed his gloves with deliberation and bowed his cue ball head. His left glove revealed a big gash filled with moon shard debris and cotton stuffing falling out. Without his straw hat, he appeared goofy. "Now, now. Disclose the truth aloud. You're embarrassed because of Shelly."

Ri lifted his hands, squeezed them into tight fists, and banged his forehead several times. "And that! Sure, bring her up! Of all the places in this town we could've landed, of course, *of course*, we end up in Shelly's backyard. The *last* person I should go near. Why was she even home and not at school, huh? Did she run home crying to her parents whining about what I did? It's bad enough that an agent from another universe is tracking us. It's bad enough that people think I *assaulted* my classmate. Oh, no. No, no, no. Let's add one more bad boy to this lineup, eh? Yes, how about we add *stalking* to my list of crimes. You know, you know, who cares if we fix this stupid universe anyway? I hope my mom doesn't get her head back. Because when she does, she's gonna *kill* me! Do you hear what I'm saying? I'm not joking here. She's gonna literally *murder* her own son and bury him in the backyard. I'm done. I'm so done. You hear me? I'm *done*!"

Rozul stood poised, his big hands folded. His glossy painted eyes glared. "It must be time for someone to eat."

Ri flared his nostrils. He wanted to scream. He wanted to punch Rozul in the chest until he smashed the plastic and wooden parts into tiny splinters. All he wanted was a friend. Someone he could share his frustration with. Instead, he was traveling with an alien manual of self-help nonsense who spouted it off at the worst times. A slow, Chinese water torture burning his brain. He growled, "Look. Starlight. Alien. Shadow Man. Can you do me one huge favor? Can you shut up?"

"Ah. So, you *were* talking to me."

Ri slapped his forehead. He whipped around. He stomped down the alley. He checked his front pocket. At least he had the cash. "We're heading to Epic Burger."

An hour later, they stood in line at the outdoor burger shack. The sun beat hard against Ri's neck. The wafting aroma of French fries and grease made his mouth salivate and his stomach growl. He stepped up to the old, dirty metal counter. The employee in the goofy paper hat chewed gum and raised a curious eyebrow.

Warren Whitman. A sixteen-year-old freshman attending Lorax Union High School and held back a couple times. Usually, freshmen were too young for the low-income early release for work program. But since Warren was sixteen, he qualified to use his last period to start his after-school job early. Ri hung out with his younger brother but never spoke with Warren. Warren's wild, curly chestnut tufts tumbled like weeds from under his dirty Epic Burger hat.

Ri gestured at the menu. "Two Epics with extra cheese and a basket of fries." He addressed his invisible looming companion. "Do you eat food? Earth food?"

Rozul dismissed him with a glove wave. "No. I absorb my energy from the sun."

"Sure, okay. Solar powered." Ri spoke to the unenthusiastic employee. "That's it."

"Nothin' to drink?"

"Nah."

He handed Warren the cash. "Hey, what time is it?"

Warren shrugged and glanced at a clock only he could see. "2:30 p.m. Shouldn't you be in school?"

Ri's eyes blazed. "Shouldn't you be putting extra cheese on my burger?"

Warren scowled and formed a freckled frown. Ri hurried up and sat down at a concrete table. An old, dilapidated umbrella failing to shield the scorching sun punctured the center. Rozul scanned the bench of the small, filthy table with narrowed brush-stroked eyebrows. He attempted to force his mammoth body into the narrow space between the bench and table. He gave up and sat on the tabletop.

A family with two young kids surrounded another table. Ri watched them out of the corner of his eye. Thirteen stomach growls later, Warren dropped the tray of food on the table with an emphatic slam. He shuffled back to the shack. Rozul pointed at Warren. "He's upset because you spoke with rudeness to him."

"Thanks, Mr. Obvious. I'll add that gem to my list of moon-shattering insights you've taught me."

"You're quite snarky when you're hungry."

Ri ripped a huge bite off the burger and chewed with his mouth wide open, spraying drops of ketchup all over Rozul. "Big bro. You've got no idea. There are reasons the bullies usually ignore me. I can shred them up verbally, from their ugly head to their ingrown toenail. Sure, they'll beat the snot out of me. Here's the win. My schoolmates will whisper my words to each other for weeks. It's verbal judo, broseph. The power of words."

Rozul fumbled a French fry with his finger and examined it like a dead fly. "What a peculiar form of energy. You shove it down the same place where you say all those mean things, and it burns for fuel. Interesting."

"Could you move your dog-pooped foot? The smell is messing up the taste of my burger." Ri had zero desire to chat. His sole interest involved chewing faster to shovel in another mouthful. He inhaled every bite, ignoring his mom's voice in his head lecturing him to slow down and chew his food.

"Too hungry."

Rozul picked at the stuffing protruding from his damaged mitt. "Sorry? What?"

Ri gurgled, his mouth too full of bread, meat, and cheese to speak. Rozul pointed and attempted to remove a napkin from the table dispenser. After a few agonizing seconds, he conceded and pushed the dispenser toward Ri.

He pointed at Ri's t-shirt. "You spilled an onion."

His left hand held a half-eaten, sloppy mess dripping down his knuckles and wrist. He wiped away the greasy slime sliding down his chin. He glanced down and studied the shiny object reflecting the sun. He dropped the second half-eaten burger onto the tray. Wiping his hands, he removed the debris from his shirt.

Not an onion—a moon shard. The same size and shape of a walnut. He gripped the sharp object, held it up high, and inspected it. The colors refracted from the dark prism. The shard contained the strength of glass or even a diamond. Heavy. Akin to the book, heavier than it looked.

"Ah. Yes. Not an onion."

Ri gripped the shard. "This means something."

"What?"

Ri jerked backward as an idea popped into his blood-sugared brain. He gripped the shard and etched a tentative mark into the sky. He predicted it would work. And just like that, he ripped a hole through the veiled air curtain, and another universe flapped with gale-force winds. The slice of a space screamed unearthly sounds.

His lips spread into a wide grin. "We're back in the game!"

15

The Irate Inspector

R I INHALED THE REST of his food, licked up all the ketchup, and gnawed off every glob of melted cheese. Then they resumed their adventure. Ri ran for a few paces. His overstuffed stomach protested with sharp jabs of revolt.

They jaunted to the nearest citrus grove, five blocks east of the residential area. Under the cover of the cool tree canopy, they devised their plan.

Rozul pointed at the moon shard. "I'm guessing when I broke the moon, it absorbed the potential to slide through another universe."

"You guess? You're not sure? Was your hat the source of all your power?"

"No. Nevertheless, I'm without my powers."

"If your straw hat isn't the source of your power, why can't you use your powers?"

"Well, the hat itself doesn't have any powers. Without my hat, I'm incomplete. And if I'm incomplete, I have no powers."

"Dude. Why do you always make zero sense? If you lost your hat, and you can't use your powers, that means your hat is the source of your powers."

"It's not so simple. The hat alone, by itself, can do nothing. It is only when combined with my head that I can achieve my will. Can your eye see without your brain? Can your brain see without your eye? Only together can you see. Is your eye or the brain the source of your sight?"

"Shadow Man, why must you inconfiscate everything? You need your hat, period."

Rozul pulled a citrus leaf from a thorny branch and sniffed. "Were you trying to say 'complicate' or 'obfuscate'? Because I heard the word 'inconfiscate,' which makes below zero sense."

Ri gritted his teeth. "Moving on. Let's take inventory. We've lost everything we need to find memories, clues, your sister's whereabouts, or the evil one who took her. We're short on intel. This moon shard gives us an advantage. Let's cut a hole into the other universe and see what we can find. This might be a great tool to outmaneuver the universal secret agent who's tracking me. Find out who they are, where they came from, and what they want with me. Or it could lead to your sister's location."

Rozul dropped the leaf, and his plastic mouth formed an O. "What? Did you misplace your marbles? What did you eat in that dead cow, mad crazy disease?"

Ri squeezed the shard harder and shook it. "Why are you acting worse than a scared Shelly? Shadow Man, *you* crossed universes to arrive here. Why you so afraid?"

Rozul wrapped his gloves around his circular head and rubbed it. Strands of stuffing stuck to it. "I made a disastrous mistake in that bungled crossing. I've lost memories. I broke your moon and lost all your adults' heads. The moon shards are ripping apart the sky. I've lost my hat. I'm awful at this! We're making a mess. And now this. The probable chances of that rip helping us are infinitesimally tiny!"

"My theory is your hat kept you calm. Why are you freaking out on me?"

Rozul lifted an invisible hat, presumably to google "freaking out." The bright painted colors of his irises melted into dismal gray. He turned around, leaned against the Minneola tree, and banged his head on a branch. "Ugh! Why's everything so hard?"

"What's up? You said star souls are good without food. I stuffed my face and now I'm fine. Whatcha need?"

Rozul wobbled around and slid down the tree trunk to the wet, grassy ground. He crossed his legs and let his head fall forward, a heap of pathetic defeat. "I'm useless. I'm defeated."

"Where's all your stupid sayings? Expect obstacles? Never despair? Keep moving forward. Chin up. Things get worse before they get better. Blah, blah, blah."

Rozul splashed open his painted alien eyes. "It sounds better when I say it. You're dreadful at cheering others up. You're a Debbie Drowner."

Ri snorted. "Got me there. Come on, though, you're an ancient alien. You're supposed to be the suppository of information."

"That sounds disgusting."

"You get what I'm saying. My therapist. My mom. My teachers. They always use those pithy sayings to morph misery into a cheerful opportunity. I'm motivated. This shard will work out awesome! Why are you shaking like a scaredy-cat? Literally an hour ago, you miniaturized us, and we flew on ants! So fantastic!"

Rozul lifted his gloved finger and formed air calculations. "Hmm, correct. Why have I given in to despair? It doesn't calculate."

"Your hat provides more than your power. It keeps you calm or something. An emotional inhibitor."

"Wow. You spoke two four-syllable words correctly."

Ri almost protested before his scalp tingled. A distant noise warned him with a hushed whisper. Air. Movement. Sound? He sensed...someone...something....

He spun around and peered down the arched tunnel of trees. His slow breathing matched the soft breeze rustling across the leaves.

Rozul's plastic mouth melted into an upside-down U. "What's the matter?"

Ri placed a forefinger against his lip. He tiptoed across the fallen leaves and overgrown weeds. He whispered, "There's someone in the grove. I hear...not sure...where...."

Rozul shouted, "Oh no!"

A surge of adrenaline sent goosebumps down Ri's arms. He whisper-yelled, "I told you to..." He trailed off. The source of Rozul's scream surfaced.

The tree sprang to life.

The branches and leaves morphed into a moving vine. They slithered at breakneck speed and grasped Rozul. The awkward alien proved no match for the threshing citrus tree. The vine leaves wrapped around his arms and legs. They pinned him to the trunk and ground with an ever-tightening grip. Ri instinctively backed away, not sure how to help. The leaves grew fast, and the branches squeezed Rozul tightly. Soon only his white round head remain exposed, his long body a vine hedge attached to the tree.

Sharp barbs crawled up Ri's leg. He kicked at them and broke free of the tentacle. Rozul screamed at him, "Run for your life!"

Without thinking, he whipped his body around and sprinted down the canopy tunnel. Another tree lashed a branch at his nose, knocking him flat. Through a partial daze, the cold ground gripped him. The constraint tightened, and thorny vine branches strangled his throat. It pulled him against the trunk and wrapped him up like his mom's vegan rice plate. Only his face—opposite of Rozul—remained uncovered.

Ri's ticker throbbed—the eerie silence of the grove buzzed.

He clutched his moon shard. The live tree limbs strapped down his wrist and arm. The silence grew unbearable. His body burned hot. His forehead sweated out droplets of instant steam. His powerlessness to do anything strangled him.

Footsteps echoed down the grove.

A confident adult strolled toward Ri and Rozul with solid steps. Each footfall planted with deliberate determination. Ri guessed at who might be approaching. The secret agent in the silver suit? Or the officer who spoke with the principal at his school? He hoped. The cop might help free them—that was what cops did, right? Help people in distress?

After an agonizing stretch of eternity, the confident adult appeared from behind a tree. A woman. The evil Librarian of Death. The Guardian Inspector. Her fractured frown beneath staring eyes pierced his soul. A black hole of space no longer concealed her head. It had been a while since Ri had seen an adult human head. But something appeared different about hers. Not human. Alien and grotesque. He gulped and squirmed. The strangling vine prison restricted his neck and chest.

The Guardian stood strong and crossed her arms. She sniffed the air—a ravenous dog tracking a piece of meat. A glowing rainbow danced within her irises—shifting winds of illumination churning. She pointed a bony finger at him. "There."

The moon shard glowed hot in Ri's grip.

The librarian approached with the same calm, slow determination. She bent over and reached across his vine wrappings, her hot breath a blowing furnace. She snatched the moon shard from his shaky hand.

Raising the shard, she pulled on her spectacles to examine the moon rock. "Ah. Yes."

She slipped the shard into her side sweater pocket. She leered, revealing her two rows of crooked and jagged teeth. A snake tongue slipped through her fangs and licked her bright ruby lips. Her raspy voice whispered, "Ssso. Should I kill you now?"

16

The Loquacious Librarian

BROKEN THOUGHTS AND IDEAS circled Ri's brain, like toilet paper waiting for an intense flush. He knew they weren't helpful. Resisting to think them proved impossible. Staring down mortal death supercharged his problem-solving, predictive power.

Why could he see the librarian's head? She was from another universe. Why couldn't Rozul talk to the citrus tree and unwrap them? Because he'd lost his hat and confidence. Why hadn't Ri cut through the fabric of space-time and jumped through *before* she had stolen his shard? Because he was an idiot.

The evil Librarian of Death spread her arms. "Oh. Forgive my intrusion into your thoughts, little Rieden Reece. Is there something more important dripping through your scrambled gray matter? Is it more interesting than me tying you up and preparing you for an excruciating death? Because if there is, please share with the class." The fingernails on her right hand turned into long razors. They grew rapidly until her right appendage morphed into a huge paw with a claw. She reached down and caressed his cheek with the tips of her razor nails.

The cold, sharp points extending from her razor nails sent shivers rippling down his skin. He growled. "How 'bout you put those scissorhands to use and cut me free so I can tell you my thoughts with my fists?"

The Librarian lifted a forefinger to her lips and feigned shock. "My, such strong words for such a helpless little boy. Tell me, you little hot pocket. Why do you choose to fight so hard? Are you not curious?"

Of course, he was curious. Madly curious. He was sure the librarian was concealing important answers. Nevertheless, he neglected to develop his diplomacy skills. Instead, all he could focus on was breaking free. And using Rozul's hidden powers to blast her back into her dark dimension.

The librarian stepped forward and leaned her grotesque head too close. She opened her reptilian mouth and inserted her long tongue inside his ear canal. He tasted a foul simmering slithering up his brain, stirring his thoughts and memories. A movie of his entire life played in fast-forward on the back of his eyelids.

She finished and yanked out her tongue—his brain sizzled. Annoying static from his grandma's old TV. The buzzing and ringing lingered.

The librarian stood straight. "See? A blank slate. Gaps and guesses; in complete darkness. You've lost important memories. Pieces missing. Incapable of explaining *why* you're even helping this big clowny buffoon." She gestured at Rozul with a dismissive wave. "He's a selfish meddler. Broke your universe, took away your mother's face. And where's he gotten you? Trapped. Beaten. Unaware of what you've truly lost."

Rozul broke his silence and croaked, "Oh so correct—old, wise, and powerful Guardian Inspector. Ri committed no crime. He only tried to help this broken shell. Take me, destroy me, or execute your righteous justice. I'm the criminal and abject failure."

The librarian dropped her head backward and roared. A deep, throaty, evil laugh echoing down the tunnel of citrus trees. "You amuse me, you deficient deviant. Oh, what has Rieden Reece named you? Rozul? Rozul, the pathetic loser." She danced around beneath the canopy, performing outlandish footsteps forward and backward.

Ri's synapses fired off a dozen ideas to connect with Rozul. His previous argument with Rozul about his hat replayed in his mind on fast-forward. Rozul had missed something important. The hat was his security blanket giving him the confidence to use his powers. That meant the hat wasn't the source of his powers; it only helped him control his powers. That meant Rozul still possessed his powers. He had simply lost his confidence. Ri hoped he was right. Rozul's access to his powers was the only way out of this.

Ri quickly calculated how to help him regain his ability to fight the librarian.

Rozul tried to bow forward—the vine wrappings prevented cue ball head movement. "Correct once again in your assessment, Oh great Guardian. I've lost. Please, respect my wishes and free Ri. He's an innocent pawn in my endeavors."

"Oh, how noble of you, the great, sacrificing Rozul! Did you forget Universal Law? I cannot acquit Rieden Reece of his infractions. He has aided and abetted an inter-universal criminal. You've undone the basic fabric of the foundational laws of this universe. He'll answer for his crimes regardless of his youth. Children are taught better than to help a shadowy figure full of mischievous uncanny powers. It's basic 101 children's rules. Stranger danger. Hello! He will offer recompense for his transgressions with his life."

As the librarian continued babbling drivel, Ri stared at Rozul, straining to draw his attention. Ri spoke inside his own mind, endeavoring to master telepathy. *"Rozul. Come in, Rozul. Open your mind to hear me. You speak to trees. Come on, focus on my thoughts. Hear me. We can escape. Access your powers, yo. Listen to me, Rozul. Use your star power. Hear my thoughts. Focus."*

Rozul maintained his argument. "I'm begging for mercy, from one old soul to another. I manipulated Ri. I used him for my benefit. He remains an innocent; he's a child. Compared to us, he has no chance—a frail human in an immature universe. Leave him alone. Take me to the Mirror of Truth. I will accept all the appropriate consequences."

The librarian flung her left hand forward, while maneuvering her two-step dance routine. It morphed into a giant paw with long claws to match her right one. She placed her razor nails together and slid them back and forth. A murderous chef sharpening her knives. "You amuse me with your pointless rambling. It's been a million years since you've updated your Universal Law database. Guardians are granted autonomy of action regarding the enforcement of preventing universes from unraveling. The Mirror of Truth sees all. If I fail to bring in this little pile of virus-meat, obligation falls on the Mirror of Truth to hold me accountable."

Ri continued to speak, directing his thoughts inside his own mind. *"Rozul. Hear me, star man. Listen up, broseph. Are you tuning into my brainwaves? Focus. Think. Harness your star power. Remember your superhero strength. You've got this. Focus. Simple telepathy, man. Shadow Man. Hear me..."*

The librarian performed her two-step dance again—a disturbed ballet dancer with amnesia. "Besides. I enjoy my work. Watching the flames of death devour this child will make a delicious memory. Charcoaled, barbequed human is a delectable pleasure."

"Wow," cut in Ri. "A cannibal? For realsies? You wanna eat a human child? I knew you were sick...that's disgusting. What is *the matter* with you?"

The diabolical librarian resumed her maniacal laughter. "Cannibal? You think this projected image you discern is my true self? Please! On this world, I resemble an adult virus-meat-monster. In my home universe, I am beautiful. Sleek. Gorgeous. And powerful. Trillions of sentient beings yearn for my power and presence. The moment will come when I devour your simple cells and tiny atoms of fragile, pathetic energy. This will not happen because I desire the flavor of your essence. No, it will display my power to those who envy my position." She pointed her razor nail claw at him. She whipped her paw backward, wincing in pain. She growled, "Why am I explaining advanced physics to a child who is too stupid to use a basic calculator?"

Ri held his face in neutral, pretending he had not noticed the librarian's pain. Had Rozul used his powers to hurt her? He hoped so. He cheered on Rozul in his mind. *"Keep going, Shadows. You're doing it. You're accessing your powers. We were wrong about your hat—you don't need it for everything. You can do this. Are you hearing me? Keep going. Get your star power back."*

Rozul spoke up again, the tremble in his voice dissolving away. "Guardian. You will do no such thing. The Mirror of Truth will agree to my terms to inflict Ri's punishment on myself and absolve him of his crimes. If I'm wrong, you can return and catch him again. He's vulnerable and powerless, no match for your great and mighty abilities."

The librarian faced Rozul and ambled forward in her usual two-step dance. She bent down and seized his cue ball head. She extended her right index claw and jammed her razor nail into his foreball. She carved a wobbly "Z" above his splashed-open eyes. When she did, a discharge of energy zapped her and she fell backward, staggering a bit.

Ri flashed a quick smile. Rozul had used his powers!

"Why did you carve a Z into his forehead?" he asked the librarian. He needed to distract her so Rozul could retrieve his bearings.

The librarian held her position and rotated her head with an owl's dexterity. Her ruby lipstick dripped like blood from her mouth. "It is the beacon code. The marker will alert the Locator to transport him to the Mirror. Now it's your turn."

Her body flipped around. No, the back of her body dissolved into the front. Ri scrunched his eyebrows together, not sure what he was seeing. She approached him and performed her two-step crazy dance.

Ri shouted in his mind, *"Come on, Rozul! You can do this! Read my telepathic thoughts, for villainy's sake. You found your powers, hear me already!"*

A soft, echoing voice replied in Ri's mind, *"I hear you. Please stop shouting."*

17

The Elaborate Escape

R I GROPED TO MASTER telepathy. He shouted, *"Did you concoct a plan? An idea to escape?"*

"Please stop pumping up the volume. I can hear you fine. Think normal thoughts."

"So—wait, what? You've been scanning my secrets this entire time? Spying on my private thoughts?"

"Hmm. This is neither the time nor place for that discussion. Let's decide how to deal with the Guardian Inspector."

"Okay, fine, whatever. Later. Shadows. Are you gonna shrink us again? Or take control of the trees? Or break her face the way you broke the moon? I'm kinda fond of that one. She's one scary psycho lady."

"I'm having difficulty calibrating my powers. My cognizance is Swiss cheese. The memories fade and return when I least expect them. For a moment, everything is clear, in focus, and then it fades away again."

"It's the confidence thing. You're losing your nerve. One minute, you can see your path clearly. Then your imagination starts freaking out regarding the danger, the what ifs, what might happen if you fail, blah, blah, blah."

Rozul's plastic painted-on eyes splashed open. *"Yes!"*

The librarian cleared her evil throat. "Ahem! Do you think I'm incapable of detecting you two idiots trying to plan an escape? Your electromagnetic thoughts are bouncing around this grove like a broken pinball machine. Pathetic. Holding on to hope with delusions of grandeur. Do you not grasp that I've won? I could kill you so fast, though it would only confuse your dead bodies. You've lost! Give it up!"

Rozul resumed his argument. "Please spare little Ri's life. He's a blameless and innocent child."

The librarian extended a forefinger paw claw. She tapped the etched Z smoldering from Rozul's head. "Save your whining for the Court of Mirrors. Given a choice, I would kill you now. Nevertheless, I've expensive credentials to preserve. The Mirror of Truth might allow me to deliver the fatal blow. Explode your atoms one by one in a fireworks display of destruction. Unlike you, I follow rules. I keep the universes tidy. I track down arrogant interlopers and sweep them into stardust where they belong."

The librarian stepped backward and froze. She grumbled and fumbled her two-step routine. She flipped her body in an impossible way. She screeched, "Stop babbling, Rieden Reece! I'm not tuned into your frequency, though I can detect the outline of your sloppy thoughts. You've lost! Failed! Give it up, already."

An idea ignited. Her ridiculous two-step dance clicked in Ri's mind. *"Rozul. I've discovered her vulnerability. Sunlight. She keeps dancing around avoiding the light streaming through the leaves. Direct sunlight hurts her."*

"Of course. It's obvious now. She probably comes from the Beta Scorpion sector in the bottom layer of Alternate Version 313. Those sentient beings are too weak to manifest native energy. They reflect it using charlatan tricks and masking signals."

"Sure, dude, whatever you say. Let's kill this vampire."

"How do you propose we do so?"

"Control the trees! Look...see the spot in the middle? That's where the trees meet above us. Wait until she walks across the center and then open the canopy. Give her a full dose of sunlight."

"Actually, it's after four p.m. on a cloudless day. If she is a few feet closer to me, we can hit her directly."

"Fine. You've got this figured out. Do it!"

"It's impolite to assert control over trees without their permission. They're creatures with feelings, thoughts, and minds of their own."

"Then talk to them, genius. Make them see our side. Ask them to help us."

Ri focused his attention on Rozul, but suddenly a razor-sharp slap stung his cheek. He hadn't noticed the librarian dancing through sunspots toward him. Her slap left him with streaks of cut flesh and a bleeding cheek. He winced, more from surprise than from the pain. Now they had a plan, though—he savored their upcoming sweet victory.

He licked his upper lip. "Nice. Blood. My favorite. Is that the best you've got? I deal with bullies every day, and honestly, you're the least intimidating person I've ever met. Unless you're ready to slice my heart out, I give you a C minus for scary."

The librarian's swirling irises darkened. She dropped her chin and glared at him over her spectacles. She stepped forward and to the side, avoiding a stream of sunlight. "If you surmise you can rile me up with your words, you're even more foolish than I anticipated. There are worse things than death. And if you give me trouble, torture is an obvious option in my hunting repertoire. Come on. Give me an excuse to make you scream with agony."

Ri stole a quick glance at Rozul. Rozul's eyes stayed shut, and if the librarian saw him, she would sense his scheming. He calculated ways to keep her distracted while Rozul communicated with the trees. Pushing back against the vine restraints, he channeled Ian Ice's personality. "Ha! Pain? Please. When I wake up in the morning, I punch myself in the face for the heck of it. There's nothing you can do to me I haven't already done. Do your worst, you vile snake vampire. Pain is my breakfast."

The corners of the librarian's mouth ticked up. Her evil eyes dripped. "I do admire your spunk. It's the rare villain I find with your tenacious arrogance. Most criminals are spineless weasels who beg, bribe, cry and otherwise act pathetic. Not you, my little meat-virus. I admire that. That's why, when I torture you, I will enjoy it so much more. There's nothing more delightful than a brain snapping from pain. When you grovel and beg me to stop, well now. There's no greater satisfaction in life. I mean it. A broken spirit? Better than pancakes."

If Ri egged her on any more, she would start acting out her threats. "Please, sista. Who ya hopin' to convince? You act tough—I see through your act. The reason you wanna torture me is simple. You feel inadequate, unqualified, and undeserving. Taking it out on me to feel better about yourself. Classic."

She snorted. "Come on. Are you even trying? That's the lamest, most inept argument you've made yet. Obviously, I love power. Power is intoxicating. And you're powerless. Being a child, you cannot comprehend how gratifying it is to control other people's lives. Power is the ultimate tragedy of free will. The cost of doing business with others. You either take it or give it away. Power is what fuels the universe."

Rozul coughed in the awkward *excuse me* kind of way.

The librarian dropped an extended paw. "What? You're interrupting our bonding moment here!" She whipped her head around and bared her teeth. "Did you discover something profound to add to our conversation?"

Rozul grinned a ridiculous grin only a plastic clown-looking creature could conjure. "It's futile to squander my words on an incompetent wannabe universal reject from the 313 sector. Talk about power. You're from the weakest energy source in all known universes."

Flames ignited in the librarian's eyes. Instead of screaming, her voice filled with darkness: heavy, low, and crackling. "It's called delicate energy. Something your privileged and obtuse race has no appreciation for. Blundering through universes with the charm and grace of a bull in a China shop. Busting up planetary satellites like chocolate chip cookies! How dare you. How dare you!"

Growling, the librarian lifted her claws high above her head. She stomped toward Rozul without dodging the light streams. Light patches touched her sweater and ignited—a magnifying glass burning through paper.

She reached the precise location, and Rozul shouted, "Stop!" His voice roared with the power of a mighty lion. The reverberations shook the leaves and shuddered his vine prison.

The librarian instinctively stopped, confusion cascading down her face.

The entire grove shook, an earthquake of California proportions.

Her confusion dripped. She cranked open her mouth wide and bared her shark teeth. She peered upward with calculating evil eyes.

The grove sprang to life, moving and quaking. Rozul's cue ball face glowed with resolute determination. The vines snapped away from his torso like cheap, worn-out rubber bands. The canopy above them shifted and churned. The leaves, branches, and thorns all slid and bent, receding. The trees shifted in abnormal directions.

The hot sunshine streamed through and blasted the librarian with direct sunlight.

Her clothes ignited and her face melted. The razor claws clanked to the grass like a spilling silverware drawer. She lifted her paws to her face to block the overpowering energy. Her body melted and burned, billowing smoke displacing her burning poison.

She screamed, and the horrific cry burned the air around her in ripples of fire and smoke.

The vines released their grip. Rozul stood up and pointed. "Run!"

Ri sprang up and bolted, his limbs a limp bag of pins and needles. The librarian hobbled away from the epicenter of the sun blast. The branches of the entire grove stretched upward—rows of tall men forming the wave at a football game. She screeched and sprinted away, leaving behind a trail of fire.

Rozul hooked onto Ri's hand, and they sprinted away. His heart pounded louder than a war drum.

18

The Revitalizing Recuperation

B Y THE TIME RI retrieved his bike and backpack from school and returned home, it was 6:30 p.m. His mom, a registered nurse at Kern County Medical, wouldn't arrive home for another thirty minutes, around sundown. He had no idea if she'd heard about his ditching, getting in a fight with Ian, or stalking Shelly. From excruciating experience, he knew this tiny town hid spying eyes and ears everywhere. The fact that a universal agent had secretly tracked him down increased his anxiety levels. The pile of unanswered questions stacked up high and weighed him down. A heavy load crushing his soul.

His stomach acid churned.

He forced himself to stop worrying. He would rather decipher world-shattering events. The broken moon, his alien friend's quest to find his sister, and their quest to dig up stolen memories all remained the highest priority. But at the moment, he needed a break.

He threw his backpack across the room at his closet door. He flopped his belly down on his mattress and spread out his arms and legs. He mumbled, "It's bedtime."

"At 6:30 p.m.? It's not even dark yet. We have so many plans to execute." Rozul waded through the room, his head almost dragging against the ceiling. He towered taller than ever. Or perhaps his missing straw hat made him loom larger.

Ri yawned. "I slept not a stinkin' wink last night. And this adventure is wearing me out. I almost died twice today. If evil librarian comes back, I gotta be 100 percent."

"Now we apperceive she's incapable of manifesting her presence in direct sunlight. That explains why she stopped chasing us beyond the library. It wasn't her human cloaking device or a need to guard the books' secrets. We must remain vigilant and not underestimate her tactics as a Guardian Inspector. She's cunning and roves about seeking to find us. Next time, we may not get so lucky charms. Oh. About reading your mind..."

Ri contained negative zero interest in Rozul's mind-tapping discovery. He squeezed his thumb and forefinger together. "Shh. It's all gravy, baby. You saved our keisters in the citrus grove. When this adventure is over, you can tell me the citrus tree's life stories too. Right now, I need sleep. You gotta leave."

"Leave? Where to?"

"Um, who cares? Why do you act so helpless all the time? Why do you expect me to think for you? You're a stinkin' star, for crying out at the horses. You're a bajillion years old. Go sleep in the doghouse. Or build a hammock between the two halves of the moon and sleep there. Shoot, go cuddle with our sun."

Rozul sat at the bottom corner of the bed, lifting the headboard up. His massive body crammed inside the bedroom made Ri claustrophobic. Rozul ignored his protest. "First of all, I require no sleep. Second, I'm wound up and want to talk. Now that I've remembered my sister, I'm bombarded with a broad spectrum of memories. I miss her. We used to stay up for years at a time talking and sharing our feelings."

Ri yawned again. He flipped his body over. He gazed at the faded glow-in-the-dark solar system stickers peeling from his ceiling. "I'm happy for you. I'm a human. Humans sleep. Without sleep, we die. I'm done arguing with you. Go away."

"You're blunt."

"Yup. Deal. You befriended an A-class jerk. How many times you gonna make me tell you to go away?"

"May I stay here in the room with you during your sleep cycle?"

"What? Like a big creeper? You gonna stare at me while I sleep? Come on, stop being a big baby. I want to fall asleep before my mom gets home, otherwise I'm busted."

"Fine. I infer I'm getting the uncooked deal. So. May I sit in the closet? That way, if you require help, I'll be nearby."

"Dude. You're huge! The closet is tiny."

"Ah, yes, see, I can expand the dimensions, stretch out the molecules. Atoms are mostly empty space. I'll shrink myself a bit."

"I guess. Whatever. Keep quiet. If I hear you making noise, you're gone, you hear me?"

Rozul's plastic painted grin dripped—a three-year-old eating a bowl of chocolates. The big Z etched into his cue ball cranium made the big clown appear extra goofy. He expanded the closet with his torn glove and crawled into the clothing crypt. He grunted, gripped Ri's old toybox, and threw it into the center of the bedroom along with other piles of clutter. After an extensive amount of rifling and shuffling, the alien powered down.

Ri changed into his pajamas. He hopped into bed, kicked off the blanket, and lay on the sheet. Yawning again, he mentally searched for his misplaced sleeping sheep. He found them staggering near a stream. He begged them to jump. Instead of leaping over their gate, they fell into the shallow stream. The cool water bubbled around their soft wool. Sheep eyes twinkled on the sly.

His eyes jerked open wide. His faculties wobbled, disoriented from extreme time loss—darkness enveloped his room. The curtain to his window remained open, and the broken moon hung unhinged. Clouds of moon shards shimmered in the clear night. Light streamed in from his open bedroom door. He sensed the familiar presence of his mother standing in the doorway, watching him.

Except now, things got worse. Much worse.

Not only did his mom have a black ball of universal space floating above her neck. Now long, dark tentacles crawled down her shoulders and arms. Pulsing tree roots, twisting and burrowing through her skin from the base of her black hole head. And the skin covering her arms and hands waned. Like a fading photograph—her body fuzzy and disappearing. The great power from the universe erasing his precious mom from existence.

Ri's body froze—paralyzed, except for his blood pumping through his veins and the sound of his heart beating against his ribcage. *No, Mom. I'm so sorry, Mom. It's not fair. None of this is fair. What's happening to you, it shouldn't be happening. It's not your fault. I'm gonna fix this. I wanna talk to you, but you're not yourself. You're not you. I'm gonna get you back. I'm gonna get your head back and your body back and fix the universe. Fix all the adult heads and the moon and make this nightmare go away. I know you can't hear my thoughts like Rozul can, but you've always had a sixth sense for what I'm feeling. I know you can feel what I'm gonna do. I can predict the future, Mom. You know that. I'm gonna fix this. I'm gonn a fix this.*

She didn't say a word. The dark tree root tentacles throbbed and gripped her arms. They dug beneath her faded skin. Her shoulders drooped, and her black hole head fell forward. The mom monster acted like it desired something important from him. A signal or word that he still cared. An impulse seized him. It prompted him to jump out of bed and approach the throbbing tentacles. But this horrific creature chilled him to the bone. He lay there, paralyzed. The rift through the universe drained away his courage. It had stolen his precious mom and replaced her with this disgusting tree monster. He squeezed his eyelids shut and imagined his real mother's smiling face. He squelched a cough and crushed down an escaping tear. He failed.

After several moments of awkward silence, his bedroom door shut. He let out his held breath. Could this imitation mother convey her concerns for him without a human head? Regardless, he refused to accept the consequences of his own actions. Saving his universe came first. Then she could toss him into the delinquent dungeon and throw away the key.

Ri pulled the sheet over his body. His mind buzzed from the increased danger. How much time did he have before he lost his mom forever? He resisted his strong urge to jump out of bed and do something. The smart part of his brain knew he needed sleep first. With trembling effort, he forced himself to locate the sheep. A dozen of them played cards and burned incense around a round wooden table. They drank mini waterfalls spilling from marble mugs. They bleated/laughed and pointed cloven hooves at each other. He urged the sheep to jump over their stupid fence. Instead, they picked up pieces of gourmet cheese and lobbed them at Ri.

At some point in the night, he must've fallen asleep, because he awoke to Rozul shaking him. "Hey. Little Jerk. It's time to wake up. We gotta pretend to go to school, otherwise your mom is gonna make you purchase a farm."

Ri twisted open a bleary eye, the memories of the day before flooding back. The nightmare memory of his imitation mom towering over him. He swallowed hard, acid churning and clawing up his throat. With the dawn of a new day, his brainpower burned clean. His fear faded into the background. Thoughts fell into focus. Ideas solidified. He envisioned the perfect plan. He predicted the future. He would save his mom with every ounce of his forceful will.

He shot out of bed. "Yup. Time to move, *now*. Let's go, not a moment to waste. We've got a planet to save, a sister to find, and librarians to kill!"

Rozul rubbed the raw Z on his forehead. "Oh. Okay, I guess?"

19

The Seductive Shard

R I SLIPPED ON HIS jeans and sneakers, sniffed his favorite shirt, and threw it in the corner. He pulled his bronze t-shirt over his head, the t-shirt his mom had bought for him at last year's Lemon County State Fair. She always cringed at the skeletons with sunglasses—it made him smirk. He plucked up his backpack, crawled through the open window, and snuck around his house. He tore away on his bike, pedaling with sore muscles.

Rozul lumbered with his backward jog beside him. "Where are we going first?"

"To school."

"That's boring."

"Sure, I got impatient yesterday. The moon had broken. I acted too hasty. Now I'm focused. We do this the right way. It's stupid to keep getting in trouble at school. And I have no way of talking to my mom about it. Did you see how much worse she is? I can't predict anymore how she might react. We go to school. I'll play nice, find a way to appease the black hole heads. *After* school we'll save the universe. It's lame. Adults are lame. They lack trust in us to do what's right. Revealing our plan to them will get us nowhere. So, we'll hide it from them. Besides, I want to find our book. It went somewhere. Hopefully someone returned it to the library or it's in lost and found. That book is important."

Rozul tossed him a circular thumbs-up. Ri curled up an incredulous lip. "Have you tried rubbing that ridiculous Z off your forehead? The librarian's tracking us."

Rozul shrugged. "I tried. She used a quite delicate signature of energy. I'm blocking the tracking signal, but removing the symbol is beyond my skill. It's embarrassing."

"Well, at least I'm the only one who can see you. Once we've retrieved our memories and restored your full powers, you can fix it then."

School grated on Ri's nerves. Not being able to talk to any adults proved more difficult than he'd imagined. The teachers tried to communicate with him—he heard nothing. Their arms and hands waved with wild circles. Pointing. Jabbing. Gesturing at the sky. Three times, he ended up facing the principal in his office. He sat there in awkward silence, unsure of what the headless adult demanded. Finally, the teachers left him alone and he sat in class, asking his classmates for his assignments. Having completed no homework yesterday, he received papers with big fat F's.

Ri shrugged it off. His priority was to save the universe by finding his missing book.

After school, he hurried through the outer gate, ready to resume his adventure. Brian Bowman waddled up, his asthma increasing the volume of his breathing. "Here. Your book."

Ri halted dead in his tracks, stirring up dust and sliding a bit. His abrupt stop caused a group of girls to almost slam into him. One giggling girl was Lisa Lemmons. She narrowed her eyes, rolled them hard, and flipped back her long mane. She pranced around him and resumed conversing with her friends.

In an instant, Lisa's graceful presence distracted him. He caught himself staring. He cranked his eyelids shut and shuddered. If one of Lisa's friends caught him checking her out, it would be game over. He shook away the annoying diversion and refocused on saving his mom.

Ri pulled Brian toward the fence, away from the mass exodus of kids. "Geek Man. What, what? You've had this the entire time? Where did you find it?"

"Well, it fell out of your backpack when you threw it at Ian. I snagged it out of curiosity. Thought with more time to study it, I could find something for you."

"Did you find something?"

"Nope."

Ri's attention caught up with Brian's statement. "Wait. What? Threw my bag at Ian?" He glanced around, half expecting Ian to pop out from behind a parked car and pound the living daylights out of him. "I didn't throw my bag at Ian."

"Uh, you did. Yesterday. When you ran away."

"Ran away?" It clicked. The moment Rozul had shrunk him, Brian, Ian, and Jimmy must have assumed he'd run away. He itched to tell Brian the truth. Tell him the story regarding Rozul and the broken moon. An exercise in futility. Brian wouldn't believe him, and he possessed a gargantuan mouth. With instantaneous gossip travel, the entire school would call Ri nuts. He had zero minus zero patience for that.

Brian giggled and smacked Ri's shoulder. "Yeah, you wimped out and ran away like a big chicken. Jimmy told everyone. The cheerleaders put you on the Not Cool Ever list."

Ri grinned. On the inside, his organs melted. He sucked in the stale air. "Oh well, you can tell Jimmy that Ian will get what's coming." He immediately regretted his response. Too late. His heart banging against a gong silenced the outer world. "I gotta go, Brian."

"Hey. Where're you going? Let me come. I'll help."

Ri harbored no ill will toward Brian. The simple fact—Brian wasn't cool. If his classmates saw them hanging out, he would end up with a nerdy group label. And Lisa Lemmons would shun him for all eternity. He shrugged. "Sorry, nothing special. Gotta clean up my room and do some more dumb chores."

Brian's shoulders fell limp. "Ah. Okay. No big."

Ri dropped a heavy hand on Brian's shoulder. "Thanks again for the book. I owe you one." Brian's face beamed, and Ri rushed away.

He and Rozul reached the far side of the parking lot and approached his bike attached to the bike stand. Someone had let all the air out of his tires and broken his plastic air pump. Ian. It had to be. Ri kicked his back tire in frustration.

Rozul's fluffy fingers rubbed his chin. "That's unfortunate."

"Oh, shut the front door, man. This is lame. Okay, Rozul, find us some transportation."

"Me? Why me? What experience do I have with travel in this universe?"

"Dude. Why do you keep forgetting your powers? Your noggin keeps resetting or something. No sleeping, no eating. You break moons. You've got the power! Come on, walking takes way too long. It will take hours."

"What's the problem?"

Ri stared up at big Rozul's Z-etched noggin. "Look at my tires! They're flat! All the other bikes are gone, and they broke my pump. The nearest gas station is a mile down the road. We've only got a few hours.

I gotta hurry up and do my chores and pretend I played video games the rest of the time. There's a silver-suited agent out there spying on me."

Rozul picked up the bike's rear tire with one glove and examined it with curious scrutiny. He scratched his chin, patted his cue ball head, and massaged the etched Z. His painted face glistened. "Ah! I've deduced. A cluster of air molecules you breathe. Simple. Crude. Effective." Rozul cracked open his wide mouth and blew out two mini tornados. They danced near his painted cheeks before jumping into the tire stems and filling up the tubes.

Rozul dropped the bike and clapped. "Problem Solvent."

Ri reeled in his dropped chin. "Now, if you could think and act that way all the time, I would have a real superhero instead of an amnesic clown." He removed the lock and chain.

"You should work on your appreciation. You're a glass-half-cracked kind of person."

Ri shrugged a dismissive shoulder and flung his leg over the bike. "Yup. You say it like it's a bad thing. Did you forget who cracked the moon? Now, come on. Let's head to that tight patch of moon shards floating over the other end of town."

Thirty minutes later, on the south side of town, they arrived at the old gas station. A tourist attraction with an ancient car and gas pumps from the 1950s. It had crumbled into disrepair along with many other buildings in town. The cloud of shards hovered above the dilapidated building like a fancy chandelier. Ri grinned from ear to ear. "Jackpot!"

Rozul mindlessly twisted the unraveled stuffing from his glove. "How do we access them? They are too high in the sky."

"There you go again, forgetting you're the most powerful being in this universe. A million ways. Stretch your arm and declare, 'Go, go, Gadget Arm,' for all I care."

"Go, go...what?"

"Shadow Man!"

Rozul rested his glove on Ri's shoulder. "You're the creative one in this partnership. I'm too inconsistent. You demonstrate a rare intellect in many universes. Sometimes I cannot keep up."

Ri frowned, unsure if Rozul was complimenting him, lecturing him, or passing him the buck. "We need another shard. How do we grab one?"

He squinted his painted peeper and peered up. "Hmm. I could lift you onto the roof of the gas station, and you could reach one from there."

"Okay, smart. Save your powers. Let's do this!"

Rozul's height, around ten feet tall, allowed him to lift Ri high. Ri grabbed the broken metal roof with chipped paint and lifted himself over. He smeared up his clothes with dirt and debris. He slid a few tentative steps across the roof—it seemed sturdy enough. Tiptoeing to the center, he targeted a low-hanging shard. He jumped several times. No luck.

His knee-jerk reflex involved forcing Rozul to help him. Did he rely too much on Rozul's powers? He could solve this one himself. He scanned the debris strewn along the rooftop and spotted a broken broom handle. He pulled it out from beneath a jumble of dusty broken shingles. He tested the stick's integrity by jamming it down on the rooftop. The stick would work.

With great care and extended jumping and stretching, he knocked the shard hard. When the stick smacked into it, a spark of electricity exploded. It blasted the stick from his grip, and the moon shard went sailing. The shard fell over the side.

Ri ran to the edge and almost slid off. From below, Rozul jumped in a way that implied he could control gravity. "I caught it! We're in the business district!"

A glint on the horizon hooked Ri's concentration. Another patch of moon shards? No such fortune. He recognized that silver vehicle. The universal agent ripped through reality.

Ri shouted, "We gotta leave, now!"

20

The Turbulent Travel

THE DELINQUENT DUO HUNKERED down inside a tiny tool shed behind the Desert Lime Museum. A decrepit and depressing museum open once a week filled with stupid tractor pieces from a hundred years ago. Why would a person with half a lick of sense pay good dollars to gaze at rusted metal? Nevertheless, the shed with the broken lock provided the perfect hiding place. The silver-suited universal agent would never find them there.

Ri held up the shiny shard. "This is our ticket."

"Our ticket to where?"

Ri punched Rozul's wooden leg. "Your hat first. So you can google Earth idioms. Your Swiss cheese brain is tiresome."

"You know where my hat is?"

"Not exactly. I've figured out this game. Energy. Telepathy. The power to pass through universes. This shard will give us access. It provides pathways or secret tunnels. I'll focus my thoughts on the precise location, rip a hole through space, and access our destination."

Rozul's drawn eyes splashed open wide. "Amazing."

Ri grasped the shard like a paintbrush. His voice trembled. "Now, don't interrupt the process. I'm focusing my cognitive function."

"What are you focusing on?"

"Hello! What did I *just* say? Don't interrupt. You lost your hat during our flying ant escape. Somewhere between the school and Shelly's backyard. She lives only a block from the school. Your hat is probably the size of lint. It's like finding a cactus needle in a haystack. I'm gonna cut a hole with the shard and reach in and grab it. It requires my complete focus."

Rozul's painted eyes swirled. "It's *my* hat."

"Fine. You focus. I'll cut the hole. Tell me when you're ready."

Rozul's illustrated eyes pinched into two spots of ink blots. He pressed his gloves against his temples and grunted. He sat motionless for an eternity. Ri focused on his own breathing. Finally, without opening his eyes, Rozul pointed his gloved forefinger.

With deft precision, Ri cut an incision down the air curtain. A dark line with flapping reality howled from a distant wind. He fissured two feet of reality. Rozul reached inside the ripped curtain and fumbled around with his big glove. After a moment, his body froze. He retracted his wooden arm with the skill of a surgeon extracting a vital organ.

Rozul pulled out his glove holding an itty-bitty straw hat. He stared at it, his painted eyes two squiggly lines. "Disappointing. It's way too small."

"Shadow Man...you're the one who shrank it! Put it on your head!"

With the hesitancy of eating anchovies for the first time, Rozul lifted the miniature hat and placed it on his colossal cranium. The hat slammed back to full size, the tattered edges rubbing against the cramped shed. He beamed. His painted eyeballs flipped with the speed of moving bars on a slot machine. The universal Google updated.

Ri peeked through the cracked wood, on watch for the universal agent. He flicked the brim of Rozul's hat. "See! What did I tell you? We'll rock this adventure in no time!"

Rozul jerked backward. "Don't touch my hat."

Ri rubbed his hands together. "Now. On to the next step. Unless there's some new insights you want to share from your crown of eternal knowledge."

Rozul's painted eyes formed slits. Then they popped open wide, three ink markings punctuating them. "I understood your reference! My hat is *not* my crown. It's my security blanket. It provides a false sense of stability. Without it, I'm lost and anxious."

"Okey doke, tough guy. Thanks for sharing. Now, the book!" Ri lifted the book from his backpack sitting on the dirt ground between his legs. "This black book is full of mysteries."

"We misplaced the memories in the canal, remember? What good is the book to you now?"

Ri banged the blank book, ready to argue. Then an idea smacked him hard. "You're right. You're right, you big, clumsy genius! We can retrieve the leeches. The moon shard portal will help us locate where the leeches ended up in what canal and where. It's pointless to comb miles and miles of canals searching for those tiny little boogers. We've got a door that'll lead us right to them. Yes! Shadow Man is back. Straw hat and the un...i...ver...sal dat-a-base!"

Ri stretched his hands up high and mimicked a football touchdown. He rubbed the cover and concentrated on the event of his lost memories. He remembered him and Rozul by the canal. The wet, stinky air rolled across his tongue and saturated his lungs. He kicked at the clods of dirt that crumbled into sand. The leeches wriggled and squirmed until they splashed into the water and swam away.

He lifted the moon shard and sliced through space. He gestured at Rozul. "Aliens first."

"That's not a thing."

"Well, now it is."

Rozul gripped his straw hat tight—interdimensional winds blew a tundra freeze through the shed. He loomed much taller than the ripped threshold. He put one leg inside and bent his torso halfway down to squeeze through. He lost his balance and stumbled backward through the portal. Ri lunged to catch him by his feet but reached out too late. Rozul disappeared.

His screams echoed from the endless void.

Ri trembled before an abyss reminiscent of the black hole heads. His bold fearlessness evaporated. Slapping himself in the face failed to help. "Man up, Ri!" He seized his backpack with his book and flung it over his shoulder. Inhaling a deep breath, he jumped through.

He lost all sense of direction and toppled over himself, falling the wrong way. Sunlight slammed against his face—he shielded his eyes while gravity grabbed him. He crashed hard against the ground on his back. It knocked the wind out of him.

He choked and coughed. A large straw hat blocked the evening sun. Rozul's painted frown and two flat lines glared. "Next time, genius, make sure you take into consideration the curvature of the earth and space. Your linear thinking almost broke your legs!" He jammed a gloved finger at the ripped curtain of space flapping in the wind ten feet above ground.

Grunting, Ri pushed himself up. "Fine. I lack your experience at tearing apart universes and traveling through them."

Rozul extended his ripped glove. Ri slapped the moon shard onto Rozul's fluffy palm. He lifted the precious instrument and shoved it under the protection of his straw hat. An unraveling finger pointed due south. "I see the reservoir right there."

Ri jumped up, brushing off the sand with renewed vigor. "Did you find the leeches?"

"Not enough time to search. Only now arrived."

"Let's go!" Ri sprinted to the fork in the canal, a small reservoir of water trapped inside a concrete cove. He reached the edge and flung his chest to the ground. He peered over the side and scanned the murky water. "There!"

A swarm of leeches congregated in the corner of the reservoir. They were treading the water with lethargic motion. They were hungry or worse, dying. He scanned his surroundings. "We need something to put them in...your hat!"

Rozul's eyebrows furrowed into two caterpillars maneuvering the inchworm. "Uh. No. Disgusting. Those things are not touching my hat."

"Fine. Whatever." Ri tossed his backpack onto a nearby mound of dirt. He jumped up and ripped off his shirt. He clumped it into a makeshift bowl/container. "Here. Hold me while I stretch."

Rozul grasped Ri's leg and dangled him over the water. He scooped out the defeated leeches and dumped them into his shirt. Once he retrieved the twenty-odd leeches, Rozul let go and he dropped to the ground, his legs crossed. He gathered up the shirt pile. His face fell.

"Snap it. Now, I gotta eat these things."

21

The Grim Graveyard

THE SLIMY AND SQUIGGLY leeches tasted sweet. Ri wanted to hurry and devour them all at once. Finish the disgusting business fast. But this required tracking them chronologically, and he couldn't lose any of the clues. So, he intended to devour them one at a time and download his experience to Rozul. His universal database could help him assemble the pieces into a clear picture.

Rozul protested, "I fail to reconcile their importance. These memories are not *our* memories. What does an annoying human boy dealing with that dangerous rat-borg, whose name I decline to mention, have to do with us? Perhaps we chose the wrong book and need to return to the library. Find a new book with more helpful memories. Memories that indeed do belong to us. Ones that do not involve us interacting with a dangerous criminal mastermind."

Ri ignored Rozul's trembling limbs. "Hey, Starshine. Get a grip. This is how mysteries work. We find puzzle pieces and fit them together. There's no point in speculating, not enough intel. Once I relive all the memories, *then* we can speculate."

Rozul flopped his jumbo body backward into the dirt, forming a smoke cloud of flying dust. "Fine. Fine. Whatever. Unpause me when you're done."

Ri dangled the squiggling leech over his mouth. Should he chew? Or swallow fast?

Swallow fast! He dropped the slimy sucker down his throat. His eyelids jerked open—he absorbed and merged with the memory.

Darkness enveloped him. Once again, his mind lay trapped inside the mysterious boy from the previous memory. The stars burned bright in a moonless sky. He desired to examine his surroundings. He could only travel by playing mental passenger within the boy's experience.

He traipsed through a lawn of sorts. Crickets chirped, frogs croaked, and a couple owls vocalized a whistling warning. The odor of dark decay coated his tongue. The boy's body flowed with lingering adrenaline. He either felt anxious in anticipation or had recently completed a dangerous activity. Ri perceived the boy's churning fear and power mixed into a deadly combination of intent and force. He savored the sensation. And recognized where the boy was walking.

A graveyard.

An unkempt, dilapidated property. Peculiar. Ri only recognized graveyards from movies, and they always seemed well taken care of. This graveyard made him wonder. He imagined the owner had died, the groundskeeper had quit, and everyone had forgotten it existed.

The boy showed no heed for the assorted sizes and shapes of tombstones. He strode forward, intent on his path. The moving shadows played tricks; the steel-nerved boy he linked up with simply thought, *Almost there.*

Where was there? Ri stayed present with the boy and ignored the eerie surroundings. The boy stopped. He turned his face to the right and placed his hands behind his back, holding his two fists together. "I smell your dirty paws."

A tall tombstone etched from cement punctured with spiderweb cracks loomed before him. From behind the stone, Belez stepped forward. The rat-cyborg unveiled his metal teeth, and the starlight bounced off them into the dark shadows. He growled, "Grim place for a meeting. If I weren't so much smarter than you, I'd assume you aim to do me in." His copper eyes glowed.

The boy replied in a harsh whisper, "You always underestimate me. If I desired to do you in, I wouldn't kill you in a graveyard and bury your rotting flesh with your fellow corpses. No. I would dismantle your empire and force you to watch your life's work burn. Forever torment you with the fact you could never claw it back. Ho-hum, what a futile effort. Someone dumber and meaner would sink to your place. There's always a dark space in every universe for your type of business. At least you keep your empire consistent and within arbitrary boundaries."

"If I didn't know you better, I'd take your back scratch for a compliment."

The boy clicked his tongue. "And, of course, you do know me better. So, my not-so-subtle backhanded compliment implied you're predictable and boring."

Belez croaked an unearthly tone. "You're likable, kid. I give you mad props." The rat jammed forward a muscle-packed paw, and the boy returned his fist bump. The rat leaned on the tombstone and interlocked his biceps. "Why here? What'd you do? What cha' need? You tastin' regret, and spinnin' second thoughts?"

"Never. In that way, we're alike. My path is clear. I stay steady."

"Even with half the universe against you? And the people you're helping not trusting you? Sounds lonely. Especially after what you've lost and the price you've paid."

"That's cheesy advice. You gonna charge me for that too?"

Belez extended his razor claws and drummed them against his bicep. "Nah. I scratch out taunts and shaming. If I offered free advice, I'd tell you to come work for me. Safer, easier, nice benefits package. Your ego's too big for the small meat sack you drag around. Would require an upgrade to your interface. You'd appreciate the amazing clarity of existence without the baggage your species labels emotions."

"Work for you?" The boy snorted. "And I thought you knew me."

"You scratch your nose a paw's grip away, scurrying around for untainted cheese. But we both scour the same sewer. Calling your business subcontracting? Tryin' to pack your own nest? Acting as an entrepreneur only paints it a different color of blood. No way you can keep your claws clean. There's only so much room in our dark tunnels of the 'verse. To build your business up requires tearing others down. Blood spills and flows down the drain. Intelligence has always been in the barter system. Impossible to get something from me without giving something up in return. In your case, it's your standards. Eroding them one compromise at a time."

The boy's stiff body planted his two feet wide apart in the grass. He relaxed and faced Belez. "Some people build up; others tear down. What I'm building not even you can comprehend. Call it compromise... I call it building strength. Strength for what is to come."

"You believe there's strength in one thought? Not every species in the 'verse is obsessed with social status and connection. That's a *human* disease. Your social structures are not strong—they're weak. Pull away one thread and it all unravels. You keep crawling to me for more tech exchange. Wasting your resources on building these fragile social networks. Trying to perfect this one thought. Thought never flows in the same direction. It's electric. Powerful. Explosive. Your work is a waste of time. And money. Let it go."

The boy's body tensed up. "I will *not* let it go. Your species infects the minority. Your dirty kind celebrate cannibalism and ripping others to shreds. Everyone that hears my business plan jumps onboard. Getting everyone to think and feel and act in the same way is pure genius. Your tech upgrades hit my goals so much faster. What might take a hundred intervals only takes one. When everyone is aligned, you will see my results. Peace, harmony, and connection. So. No. I will not let it go. *You* let it go, broseph. Now, are we done with the chit-chat? Are we making the deal or not?"

Belez lifted his claw and tapped a metal tooth. He pointed. "Making me ask questions, I despise that. Why you forcin' my grip?"

Beneath a pocketed layer of the boy's mind, he complained, *Why does he always play this weak offense?* "You're wondering why I trust you? No harm, no foul. My intel suggests a third-party hacker with no connection to you. Besides, rebuilding my face after that weak explosion took five subunits. I doubt the interference came with the intent to kill me. Discourage me, more likely. Wasting my time and money, nothing more."

The rat rested against the tombstone and scratched his claws along the broken chunks of concrete. "And?"

"And you wonder how I got the intel. Trust me, it's not anyone in your organization. No planted mole inside your association. That's suicidal poisoning, since you rodents never play nice."

Belez pulled his long nose up and cackled, saliva dripping down his metal teeth. "Please. Infiltrating my team caused no serious itch. Most people wouldn't spend a moment with your filthy kind. Not to mention sympathizing with the pathetic cause you're fighting for. No. That's *not* my insinuation."

Synapses misfired inside the boy's brain. He grappled to pinpoint the rat's implication. "What? What are you afraid of?"

The rat's sneer cracked apart. "Careful, punk. I enjoy our banter, don't 'chew dare disrespect." The boy forced a half-nod, an inner turmoil raging, heating up his blood. "Belez. I use my brain. Our exchanges benefit you. I'm not using a hacking system, a mole, or any other intrusive measures to calculate our chess moves. Why kill me? What, someone paid you a good sum to plan an attempt? You view me as a credible threat? Besides, even if you tried and somehow failed—and failure is *so* unlike you—who else is going to deal with me? I can take chances, too. I can take care of myself."

The boy's heartbeat hammered hard inside Ri's mind. He detected the boy's lies. He couldn't discern whether the rat believed them.

Belez shrugged. "Fine. Stories. Tall tales. You live in your fantasy world—dreamer, eh? It offends me you're so cavalier with an underbelly threat. Each species has their quirks. If you wanna brush it aside, I'll let your indiscretion slide. And if you refuse to challenge me, I guess you can avoid the bait. That type of behavior, young buck, will get you exterminated by the grand spectators. Most places and most universes label such weakness."

"You know I'm not weak."

"Which concludes confusion. You humans are self-destructive. I share free intel for you to stay on guard. There exist death-dealing powers and poisons beyond my protection. My pack alliances use clever bait and lead to traps. You're not high enough on my food chain to lose my share. But I respect your tenacity. I forgive, this time. Next opportunity, provision to keep secrets becomes a luxury. Now, let's retire this convo."

"Where is it?"

"You're favorite spot. Entropy. Requires a nice dig, like an obedient pet." The rat bared his shiny teeth and melted into the dark.

The boy scanned his surroundings and strutted through the graveyard. The insects grew louder, and the dark shadows danced. He disrespected the graves and leaped across open pits. Heaps of dirt covered some graves. The abandoned graveyard's dilapidated condition screamed utter despair and loneliness. A deep shiver shook down Ri's spine.

The boy stopped and dropped to his hands and knees. He pulled a small metal rod from his pocket and waved it over the ground. The rod projected a small laser dot over an area of the grave. The boy dug in the soft, wet dirt. A couple inches under, he pulled out a plastic container that fit inside his cupped palm.

A moment before the memory dissolved, the boy glanced up at the tombstone. A cold chill gripped the otherwise fearless boy. His gaze locked for a second, and he recoiled. The name etched into the tombstone read: *Rieden Reece*.

22

The Perilous Path

R I'S EYELIDS FLIPPED OPEN, and his breath shot out in shallow rips. Cold sweat and an eternal chill gripped his limbs.

Rozul's plastic painted face dripped with worry while he shook Ri's arms. "What is it? What's wrong? Are you dying from dermis disease?"

Ri's consciousness boomeranged back to his current reality. The separation from the bold and fearless boy jarred him. He seized Rozul's thin arms and growled, "I'm dead. I'm dead."

Rozul's face melted hot colors, and he bobbed his cue ball head backward. "You're dead? What do I do? Defibrillate your heart?" He raised his glove high with electricity crackling between his finger and thumb.

"What?" Ri slid backward in the dirt. "No. Not now. I'm alive right now, ding-dong. The memory! The boy, the rat, the graveyard! Is it the future? Are these future memories?"

Rozul snatched up a squirming leech from the pile. He examined it incredulously as if searching for a date stamp. "Hard to tell. Don't recall memories ever manifesting in this specific way." He dropped the leech back into the pile. Shifting his hat sideways, he retrieved the shard and held it out, cradled in his glove.

Ri grabbed the shard and shoved it into his pocket. "Man, Shadows. These memories are messing with my head. I have no clue who this mystery boy is or why I'm reliving his memories. He's building some sort of alien high-tech connection-based network. Like a Google that controls your thoughts or something. There's something so familiar about him. The way he said: 'Let it go, broseph.' I've heard those words before. Somewhere. I'm not sure. He's connected to all of this, somehow. I need to figure this out. How much time do we have, you think?"

Rozul pointed at the sky. "I've conducted some series calculations while you wasted away your time with criminal memories. If we don't find my sister fast, the disassembled moon and cracked universe will achieve complete entropy. We can no longer fix it."

"What? No! Well then, how much time do we have left?"

Rozul's painted mouth split open to speak—a nearby noise kept his mouth propped open.

A strong wind picked up, blowing dirt everywhere. Ri whipped around, imagining a helicopter ready to land. No. Much worse. The universal agent! And the silver-suited seeker of death arrived in an upgraded ride. Some sort of alien spaceship with flame tires hovering a foot above the ground. Beams of circling scarlet and bronze lights vibrated. They swirled across the extremity of the alien technology. The roaring engine deafened him. The gale force rippled the canal water.

The silver-suited agent leaped from the spaceship. An elephant-sized dual-barrel rocket launcher balanced on the agent's shoulder. The agent jumped twelve feet and landed hard, driving one knee into the dirt. They aimed the weapon straight at Ri's forehead. He backed up, his perception of time slowing down from the adrenaline spike.

Ri shouted, "Stop! Don't shoot. Let's talk about this...."

Rozul jumped between Ri and the agent, his limbs dangling in odd directions. His huge hands fell on the agent, and they both tottered. Ri—paralyzed—watched a stray blast from the agent's cannon hit the reservoir gate. It exploded into jagged chunks of molten metal. The liquid mercury flowed into the rushing water and sizzled into a cloud of steam. Ri stepped backward, unsure if he should venture to help or run for his life.

Rozul and the agent grappled, falling at a painful angle. They wrestled. Rozul displayed great strength and speed, unlike his usual lumbering self. The agent thrust powerful punches and fought with a fierce grace. Blow after blow, the agent pounded Rozul's ping-pong ball head, beating in rows of dents. In the scuffle, the agent pushed him backward and they both landed on the pile of leeches. The leeches exploded, spraying bits of blood and slime everywhere.

Rozul flipped a glance at the squished leeches. The agent whipped out a fluorescent emerald dagger from inside the silver suit. He pushed the agent's fist away—the agent moved too fast.

"Run, Ri, run!" shouted Rozul. "Use the shard...."

The agent's grip overpowered Rozul. The fluorescent blade seared through his chest, ripping through his plastic and stuffing. He screamed; a haunted echo from an ancient universe cracked. The sonic shock wave toppled the agent backward, slamming them into the spaceship.

Rozul lay on his back, the glowing hot blade protruding from his chest. He hoisted his trembling glove to point—his hand collapsed.

The agent regained their composure and rushed forward again. The agent towered over Rozul's fallen body. Their black hole head grew ominous and dark with lightning exploding above their neck.

The black hole head rotated—though it revealed only darkness, the agent's focus burned hot. The memory of Rozul's words echoed in Ri's mind: *Use the shard.*

The agent leaped forward and lifted a small glowing rod from their suit. Ri stepped backward and slid his hand into his pocket. He held the shard—hot and sweaty in his palm.

The agent pointed their weapon. Ri whipped the shard from his pocket and dove sideways at the dirt road. He scratched a quick portal into the air, and the jagged edges flapped from a dark universe. A jumbled jump through—the laser blast scorched the seat of his pants.

He dropped into the darkness with no focus on location.

He somersaulted and hit the ground hard. Daylight melted into midnight. No longer near dry desert dirt—the wet blades of grass tickled his skin. An unusual warmth from the bright starlight soothed him. The insects whispered in synchronized harmony. This place seemed familiar.

The graveyard. His torso shot up straight, a new sensation gripping him. He glanced around the darkness without adjusted eyes. Shadows and crumbling tombstones played with his imagination. Had he arrived at the *same* graveyard? How could he be here? When was here? In the past, present, or future?

The image of the etched tombstone with his name surfaced to mind. That would at least tell him his location. He pushed himself up, wary of some stranger lurking in the shadows. Would he find the boy? Or worse, Belez? He treaded the graveyard with nimble precision, avoiding stepping on graves. Some might call it superstitious. He imagined himself dead in a grave. The idea of people stepping all over him stiffened his neck hair.

He followed the path in his memory and located his bearings. The tall tombstone to his right. The tiny plastic one up on the left. A slight curve of the hillside. The mound of dirt. The exact same layout. Soon, he found it. His tombstone.

He knelt on the ground next to it and traced his etched name within the crumbling concrete. Date of death: *October 13, 2020*. Thirty-two-years old, in the future.

The insects fell silent. A soft creeping approached, disturbing the still night air. He caressed the shard in his pocket, his grip on hair-trigger alert to jump through a portal. His body held stiff while tracking the creeping with an outstretched ear.

His own loud breathing screamed. The echoes from the footfalls grew louder.

His worst nightmare came to life. Belez, the cyborg-rat, stepped out from behind a tombstone. The starlight reflected off his metal teeth, his dirty saliva sliding down his snout. He resembled a rabid dog itching to attack. The rat's lip curled up. "Well, well, well. Something wicked this way comes. What role do you play? A novice spy? Not so friendly tip: dress the part. You look like you've been playing at a carnival. Not sneaking through a graveyard at midnight."

Ri took one shivering step back and steadied himself.

The rat extended a razor nail. "You're rattled. Unexpected trip? What are you sniffing at, boy? What brings you here? Answer me! I can strangle you without effort, vermin. On the other paw, one manipulates pivot points in time delicately. Who are you and where's your insight at?" The rat tapped his temple, the echo of metal on metal.

Ri struggled to speak. The rat's vicious gaze paralyzed him.

The rat advanced. "I smell naivety. So young. Mentally, I detect. This is beyond you. Why meddle in affairs you shouldn't? Boredom. Melancholy. Childhood mischief a curious step too far?"

Ri bristled at the word "child." His brain worked a step faster than most. His experience paled in comparison to Belez, though he could match wits with anyone. He pointed his trembling finger at his tombstone. "I came here to find out why I died in the future." The best lie sprang from an unbelievable truth.

The rat narrowed an evil eye, the copper glow intensifying. He followed Ri's gesture and studied the tombstone. One of the rat's eyelids flapped open, a runaway window blind. "What? This is you? You are Rieden Reece." The rat almost whispered his name.

"Yes."

Belez did something unexpected. He chuckled. "Oh. How. Now. This is tasty. Little Rieden Reece. Curious. You're such a scared little boy. I hear fear is a great motivator for fueling rage. You humans and your tenacious emotions."

Ri's shaking stopped. The cool air no longer chilled him to the bone. His mouth twitched an attempted protest, but then something stopped him dead. The ominous tombstone disappeared.

The rat waved his claw through the empty space the tombstone used to occupy. His copper eyes burned with fire. "What? You humans are cockroaches! Changed in one bite? Does time mean nothing? How dare you! Lifespans of insects, yet you can slip through time without consequence."

The rat flicked his razor nail forward. "I will kill you now, erase it all!"

Ri stepped back, his finger caressing the shard. Why had his tombstone disappeared? That was a good sign, he hoped. But first, he needed to get away from Belez before he changed his death date to today.

Another voice from the darkness whistled from an eerie wind. "Not yet, Belez. Wait until the loop is complete. This is one prediction."

The voice sounded familiar, high-pitched and dangerous. A petite shadow emerged from the twilight, her spectacles reflecting the starlight. The librarian formed a nefarious smile. "He's a scared little puppy. Worry not, he will die when time has solidified."

The librarian's voice punctured the cold wind and sent icicles down Ri's back. His body tensed, now forced to deal with double trouble. His trembling fingernail scratched at his moon shard.

Belez jammed an extended razor nail at Ri. "What do we do with him now?"

The evil librarian placed her hands behind her back and sneered wickedly. "Now? Now we torture him."

23

The Fantastic Fake

TIME EXPANDED AND SLOWED. Ri's eyes narrowed in on the danger with pinpoint accuracy. The evil Librarian of Death advanced, and he did not hesitate. His visual cortex concentrated inward on a precise where and when. He yanked out the shard in his pocket and sliced through the curtain of existence.

The rat lifted a weapon from his leg. Sunlight streamed through the portal, striking the librarian like a whipping rope. She screamed a bloodcurdling cry as the light burned her fabricated skin. She stepped backward too fast and tripped over Belez. They both stumbled and intertwined.

Ri shouted, "Suckers!" He leaped through the portal.

Belez fired a laser shot, striking the edge of his earlobe. Ri twisted in an odd direction and crashed through the rip in space-time. The instantly bright sunlight temporarily blinded him. Losing balance, he collapsed into the sand.

Hot, ugly dirt! He lay on the ground with his eyes closed, waiting for them to adjust. After a few seconds, he risked a glance. Sure enough, he'd arrived exactly where he'd intended. Across the street from his house at the south end of little Fenway Park, near the trees and sidewalk. He pushed his aching body up, put the shard back in his pocket, and brushed himself off. An earlobe caress ignited a sizzle, shooting a searing bolt down his neck. He needed a shower and to wash his clothes before his mom came home.

Ri looked both ways and almost crossed the street—a familiar rumble interrupted him. The loud electric hum crackled along the stiff breeze. The energy displacement from the universal agent's spaceship tingled his extremities. He ducked back underneath the mesquite tree and peered out from behind the twisted trunk.

A moment later, the monstrous ethereal machine dove down and hovered near the entrance of his house. Why did the agent have to be arriving now? His mom finished work around dark, close to seven p.m. What horrific thing was the agent planning for her? Did the agent intend to set a trap?

Thirst and fear clawed at his throat. He waited and watched, eager to unlock the agent's next move. The roaring motors and scorching heat generated from the spaceship garnered absolutely zero attention. The nearby strolling black hole heads ignored the vehicle monstrosity. Oblivious, they continued doing their own thing. No doubt the ship utilized a cloaking device, invisible to the broken adults.

A latch opened, and a strong beam of energy escaped from inside the spaceship. The shiny-suited agent stepped out into the open air. An unknown force lowered the agent via an invisible escalator. The agent whipped forward a massive laser cannon, balancing it on their shoulder. They marched around the spaceship and headed for Ri's house.

A faint whisper penetrated his mind. *"Hey there. It's me. Can you hear me?"*

He glanced around to ensure he was hearing the telepathic voice and Rozul wasn't nearby. *"Yeah. Shadows. You okay? Where are you?"*

"*The universal agent captured me. I'm in the spaceship and gravely wounded. I require advanced medical attention. My alignment is off, and I've no energy access to fix myself.*"

The spaceship shimmered and shined in the sunlight. Fiery flames licked orange swirls around the base of the hovering hunk of metal. No windows, portals, or methods to peer inside. "*What can I do? How do I get you out?*"

On the rear of the ship, a section of smooth silver turned translucent. Rozul's dented cue ball face cracked a faded smile. "*My ideas come in chunks. I visualize a plan. I can stretch metal. Your backpack is here. I can shrink down to size of backpack. You come get me. The energy expenditure will make me lose connection.*"

A loud explosion erupted. Ri stretched around the tree and tracked the agent. The agent blasted a gaping hole through his living room wall. He groaned. *Well, that's just great.* How would he ever explain that to his mom?

"*Hurry!*" Rozul yelled within choppy telepathy. "*I'm losing control!*"

Ri waited until the agent entered the rupture of burning wood, metal, and glass. Then he sprinted across the road, forgetting to watch for oncoming cars. He reached the thin metal area on the spaceship where Rozul had dispersed the atoms. His face—a busted-up cue ball, paler than a plate of white rice. He shrank himself, a large lumbering alien shriveling down to the size of a small cat. Ri stuck his arm through the warped, wavering hole. The dancing atoms raised his arm hair and sent a tingling sensation up his shoulder. He lifted tiny Rozul and cradled him in his arms.

Rozul coughed. "*Put me in the bag. Hide me.*"

Ri whispered aloud, "No chance. You're barely alive." The orange energy flames licked at his legs, so he moved fast, holding Rozul like a bird with a broken wing.

The universal agent jumped out of the living room and sailed through the air, landing ten feet away.

Ri slid the shard out of his pocket. Like a ninja wielding a star blade, he sliced through the fabric of space. He stepped through it sideways just as the agent spotted him. He allowed the agent a second to advance, a second to believe they might capture him.

Ri held on to his friend with a tenacious grip. This time, he managed to step through to the other side without plummeting. His backpack slammed into the wall of the area he transported himself into. Sliding downward, he sat hard after banging his head against the ceiling. He rested, cross-legged, holding Rozul. His body swayed from the quick transfer of location.

Bess, the family dog, sniffed at the mini alien. Bess licked Ri's cheek and burnt ear. She tilted her adorable pit bull face sideways.

Ri whispered, "Good girl. We'll stay hidden in your doghouse until the universal agent is gone. The agent would never suspect we traveled so close."

Bess groaned. She rested her nose on Ri's knee and whimpered. Rozul spoke via telepathy, *"It's too difficult to hold this size much longer. I need the frog."*

Ri squinted in the dark, cramped doghouse. "What?"

No response. Rozul fell unconscious.

24

The Hopping Hospital

MINIATURE ROZUL VIBRATED IN Ri's hands. It started with a slight shaking, which graduated to a rhythmic pulsating. Soon Rozul was trembling with a condensed energy pulse blistering his hands. Ri's eyes cranked open wide. He jumped backward, hitting his head hard on the roof of the doghouse. Ri dropped Rozul and screeched at Bess, "Run for it!"

Bess and Ri sprinted from the doghouse. Ri's wild running kicked up so much thick dust he almost tripped over Bess. A second later, Rozul exploded. With a thunderous crash, he expanded to his original size. His ginormous frame loomed much larger than the doghouse.

Bits of wood, paint chips, nails, and sawdust blanketed Rozul. An unconscious alien lying on his back with doghouse remains decorating him. Bess chewed on some spilled dog food lodged in Rozul's armpit.

Ri grumbled and took out his frustration on the dog. "Knock it off! We gotta get this goober inside. Hang on, though. First I gotta make sure the agent is gone. All this racket could've woken up the dead."

Tiptoeing to the front of the house, Ri peered around the corner. He marched around the house's perimeter to make sure the coast was clear. No sign of the agent. He needed to figure out who this agent was and how they were tracking him. But Rozul came first.

After removing all the debris, he and Bess managed to drag the oversized alien back into the house. Mostly Ri. Bess continued to play tug-of-war with Rozul's already damaged body. Luckily—and not so luckily—for Ri, the silver-suited agent had blasted a Rozul-sized crater through the front of his house. This made it much easier for him to drag a cumbersome, unconscious alien inside.

Once Ri dragged him inside and hoisted most of his body onto the bed, Ri collapsed. Somewhere in the depths of his awareness, a strong mixture of overpowering emotions knocked. They demanded entry. Little nasty booger blobs of anger. He could choose to dwell on the destroyed house and doghouse. He might imagine how his mother would react when she got home from work. How to explain that he'd misplaced his bike again. He yearned to guess the sliver agent's next play. He needed to find the mystery boy who had visited his future gravesite. That boy had key insights into their lost memories. They also needed to find Rozul's sister—and they still had no clue where to start.

He could contemplate failing his mission and never fixing his world. Enduring living the remainder of his life in a broken universe filled with adults comprised of black hole heads. Growing up and becoming an infected adult. Never seeing his mom's face again...

He sighed, loud and long. Nope. He gave no such permission to his anxiety. First fix Rozul. Find help. Once Rozul recovered, then he could fall apart. *Not* before.

How would he fix his ginormous companion? He had mumbled madness regarding a frog...for what? To eat? Did the frog contain healing properties in his universe? He remembered Bess licking the toads by the canals. Their skin would make her act berserk. Drugs for dogs or something. Toads and frogs—not the same, though.

A small red light flashed from under Rozul's right glove. Ri lifted the fluffy palm and flipped it up, somewhat. Maneuvering the collapsed body exhausted him. A flashing light pulsed within the center of the dirty glove. Should he press it? Ri's finger hovered over the flashing red button. Ri frowned and his mind locked in hesitation. It had to be something important, right? Was this how a star alien answered a phone call? Ri closed his eyes and gritted his teeth. He held his breath and forced himself to press the flashing red button. There was only a fifty-fifty chance they might explode.

A three-dimensional image solidified above the glove. A mossy head with big eyes sprang to life trapped in an upside-down cone display. A growly voice shouted midsentence, "...accept the charges or not? Quick rate by the nanosecond here. You're getting billed for this connection. Am I on my way or not? Got a full charge in my Jump-Pad. Am I coming or not? Make your decision, a yes or no. My tongue isn't getting any sharper."

Ri hesitated and his voice cracked. "Er. Um. Frog? I guess we need your help."

"You guess? You guess?" The frog's bulging yellow eyes doubled in size with laser focus. One eyeball swiveled sideways and scrutinized the unconscious Rozul. "*You guess* doesn't fix your friend, does it, young mammal? Let me break it down for your simple cerebrum. Death. Or money and life. Bum, bum, bum. Those are nanoseconds croaking. You got the greens; I got the means. You acquiesce?"

Ri's head bobbed. "I got the greens." He pretended he understood. "And I abisence."

The frog's bulging eyes expanded even larger, blocking the view of his head. "Show me the greens."

Ri stalled. "No time! He's good for it, frog sir! Look, nanoseconds are running out... What, did he stop breathing? Hurry up!"

The frog's head zipped back and forth. "Right. Breathing? Stars don't breathe...oh, vibrating, you mean. Hang on, I'm on it. Now, where did I put those Jump-Pad keys...." The frog strolled out of view and the projection disappeared. An empty hovering cone of static imagery buzzed without an image.

Ri waited.

And waited.

He expected the frog to return—he stared at the silent transmission of nothing for endless ages.

The bedroom nook exploded. A walloping rip in time and space expanded outward, and the energy from another universe roared through his room. The blast knocked him down and shook everything loose. The edges of the wormhole rippled with inside-out clouds of energy pulsating. In the center, a muscle-stacked frog propped up on his hindlegs surfed in on a gold-plated metal disk. He leaped from the entrance and balanced at the base of the bed, flexing the many layers of muscles on his arms. He hooked the hovering disk and tucked it behind his back. The wormhole closed in on itself, and the thunderous roar ceased to overpower the room.

"Was that really necessary?" said Ri, taking in the damage and wincing.

The frog pivoted a bulging eye, examining the corner where he'd entered. "Cut that too close, eh? Calibration on my pad is crabby. Gonna get that glitch stitched. What are you staring at, meatboy? It's *your* nanoseconds."

Ri grabbed the frame of his bed to pull himself upright. The frog stood only three feet tall, but his buff stature screamed intimidation. He only wore cut-off blue jeans. His chest muscles and bodybuilder abs rippled. Ri coughed. "Uh, he used up too much energy, or something. The universal agent stabbed him in the chest. He's unconscious."

The frog stretched its webbed fingers wide—a musician starting his rock concert. He rippled his digits and expanded the suction cups with stretching maneuvers. An endless array of medical instruments and three-dimensional displays swelled into view behind the frog. A mechanical arm extended and rested sparkling goggles in front of his bulging eyes.

The frog croaked, "Meat machine. I can read your thoughts. What universe do you imagine I hail from? My name is not frog. That's an acronym. It stands for Freelance Reconnaissance and Operations Guru. Emphasis on the guru. I've registered a million plus names though. I pick a novel name for each new universe. This is the first time I've traveled so far to work in such a dump. The air smells of swamp. Everyone's molecules stay bonded together like a depressed teenager's will to live. The light is weak and bent. The decay is in my teeth, and I can taste it on my tongue." The frog snapped its long tongue out several times, cracking electricity. "Yuck. I forgot to bring my filter suit. The website for this solar system lied. Free Wi-Fi, give me a broken fried leg. My tadpole nephew could poop out better technology than what's pumping apart this planet. Embarrassing. I'm embarrassed for you. Genuinely."

"Way to be judgmental."

"Oh, thanks. Not expecting compliments from a meat-brain."

Ri waved both hands at him. "Are you going to heal him, or what?"

The frog leaned forward and smooshed his bulging eyes into Ri's personal space. "Ho there, the name is not frog. No. I randomly choose...Nico. Yes, Nico. Nico? Yup. Nico. How does Nico taste on your native tongue?"

"Um. Fine. I guess. Does it mean anything?"

"Mean? Oh, meaning. Well, yes, it's irrelevant. It means I am the Greatest and Most Powerful One and Supreme Director of All Importance and Bringer of Knowledge to Universal Harmony with Strength of the Atomic Protector. Oh wait, whoops. That's the unconscious guy's name. Huh, what does Nico mean?" Nico tapped his goggles with a suction fingertip. "Ah, it doesn't matter. Now, what I am doing?"

Ri rubbed his weary face. "Nico. Doctor. Dude. Whatever you are, fix Rozul!"

The hundreds of alien instruments expanded behind Nico. He stretched his strong arms wide. "Correct. Thanks, meathead. I'm not a doctor. I'm an *operator*." He croaked the word with a deep growl, though the importance of it fluttered and fizzled. Lightning cracked between his webbed digits. Hundreds of arms extended, holding an unfathomable array of other-universe tech. They hovered above Rozul. Dozens of devices whizzed forward, connecting with the blacked-out body.

The frog's eyes bulged three times bigger inside the goggles. He stared with fierce concentration at a couple dozen three-dimensional screens. Covered by numbers and spinning variables, the nonsensical details induced dizziness.

Rozul shook. He vibrated and sparked energy in random directions. His torso jumped with violent convulsions. His chest heaved and his limbs flailed. Robotic arms jammed him with dark patches of gravitational force.

He shook with such violence that Ri was terrified he was about to explode. Ri covered his eyes and backed into the corner of his room. "Nico! You're gonna kill him!"

Nico shouted above the loud roar, "Possibly!"

A force field spherical beam of energy formed around Rozul. Inside the field, half a dozen robotic arms overheated and exploded. He caught fire. But the fire did not burn in an ordinary way. Flames from the hottest furnace burned bright. Heat from the fusion generator of a giant star generated exponential levels of power. The intense heat became overpowering. Ri almost passed out.

Rozul exploded inside the force field.

Nico lifted his goggles and protruded an inquisitive eye bulge. "Whoops."

25

The Qualified Quark

I T REQUIRED A DOZEN false starts, explosions, and strings of expletives from the frog doctor. Plus one long, silent pause. Rozul's chest expanded, and his painted eyes splashed crashing waves. He shot up straight and stared past them at some unspeakable horror.

The bed collapsed. Ri cringed. His comic books and video games were piled in a stack under his bed. He rushed forward to check on Rozul, but one of Nico's robotic arms grabbed him and held him back.

Rozul seized his electrified hat. Both of his frayed gloves smashed against his beat-up head. His painted lips cracked open and foreign utterances spilled out.

An odd grimace danced around Nico's face, his long tongue zapping the air absentmindedly. "Got this. Got this," he mumbled to himself. He rapped away at the three-dimensional controls with his webbed digits. Ri flexed his hands, waiting. Watching the seconds tick by on his Men in Black wall clock.

Nico's equipment worked with speed and precision. The robotic arms and zaps of gravitational energy rejuvenated Rozul. The etched Z on his forehead glowed several colors and faded. A needle and thread stitched up his ripped glove—it glowed snow white. The frayed edges of his burnt straw hat regrew themselves, pushing out new straw from the center. The debris covering his wrinkled body and clownish alien suit drained away. The dents all over his curved head popped out one by one, and a mechanical arm with a squeegee wiped on a smooth shine. Ri grinned from ear to ear. This was working. He would get his Rozul back.

Rozul radiated. Golden rays emitted from his body and every scratch, tear, and rip disappeared without a trace. No scars. No damage. He appeared freshly manufactured from an automated assembly line.

His nonstop string of strange sounds translated into English. "...not since the all-millennial party at the Universal Governor's mansion!"

Ri rushed up to him, his alien body low from resting on a crushed bed. Ri wrapped his arms around him and squeezed hard, hugging him tight. The warmth radiating from his new and improved body generated calming waves. "You're alive! This crazy frog saved you!"

Nico's eyes bugged and beamed. "Aw. No big. Sure, yeah, I'm extra crazy. Wait, crazy is good, right? Because I'm totally that."

Rozul pushed Ri away so he could stare into his eyes, gripping his shoulders. "Brother from another 'verse, I've got so much to tell you!"

The frog retracted thousands of robotic arms, mechanical limbs, and three-dimensional molecular manipulators. During the hovering hospital's retreat, Nico beamed. He babbled, "Ah. His coded calibration cracked. Hard to swallow how his superposition remained stable in this undeveloped universe. His fragile padding protecting his inner star power from going big bang supernova. Pollywog basics. Been doing this since tadpoles went through their uncool stage. Lucky I had an opening. Booked up for a solid year, though there's always time to sing in chorus for an old friend's distress call."

Ri nodded with great vigor, pretending he understood the crazy frog jargon.

Rozul caressed his straw hat, which was emitting golden rays. "I owe you."

"Yup! A lot! Now, about those greens." The automated hospital retreated to the invisible plane of space it occupied. Only the buff frog with a rucksack remained. He extended his webbed palm and waited.

Ri gulped and forced an awkward grin. "Ah, ha. Yeah. About that. Rozul...?"

Rozul held his smooth chin with a bright ivory glove. "Did you lie?"

Ri groaned. "Seriously? You're gonna give me a guilt trip? I saved your life! Well, I mean, I pushed the red button, said the right words, and frogger friend saved your life. Gratitude, alien dude!"

Rozul placed a white glove on his hip. Nico placed a webbed hand on his hip. They both stared with incredulous, disappointing parental stares. Rozul lifted his glove and swirled his finger, a burst of golden energy dispersing into ripples. "You've forgotten. Your access to funds. With your mom's checkbook. And the pen I loaned you."

Ri jumped up and ran to his backpack in the closet. He fumbled around and pulled out the checkbook. He tried not to think about how he might explain this to his mom. As a nurse, she understood hospital expenses. But a quark frog doctor from another universe? Ri shuddered. He shook away the vivid image of her black hole head and tree root arms reaching out to strangle him. He ripped out a blank check and waved it at Nico. "How much?"

The frog snatched the blank check. A mini magnifying glass appeared from the side of a metal band fused into his head. His bugged eye peered through it. "Ho, there! Nice currency. Antiquated. Sorry, not sorry, refusing this form of payment. You said greens!"

He waved the blank check back at Ri and dropped it at his feet.

Ri offered a lopsided grin. Rozul grunted, "Now that my calibration is correct, I ascertain an obvious pattern with you, little spark. I can't solve all your problems."

Ri formed a polite smirk at Nico, the way one smiles at an adult right before they devise a way to outsmart them. He caressed the shard glowing hot in his pocket. Calling his name. Ready to slice a new portal so they could ditch the frog. Ri jerked the shard out and was making the motion to cut the air when Nico's lightning frog tongue snapped out. The long steel wire wrapped around Ri's wrist—he lost his grip on the shard. Nico hopped forward, and the shard dropped into his webbed digits.

He pulled the shard in close and used the magnifying glass to scrutinize it. Nico caught his breath. "Well, in all my billion plus years, I never. This is beautiful. Made of our same energy. A quark. Check, check this design. More elegant than diamonds. The gleam of it." Nico continued to mumble to himself.

The swirls of Rozul's painted face shrank. "Ah, yes. Unintended consequence of my universal breach. I kind of broke their planetary satellite. We've been working on getting it fixed."

The frog stumbled around the room in a careless meander. He stared at the shard with fixed fascination. "I've never seen such a manifestation of matter. This is the same quark energy found in our universe. Yet, fused. With the simple structures bonding this young and boring system. It's elegant. Powerful. Creative. Fantastic."

Rozul gestured a sweeping move with his glove. "Does it cover our expenses? Because there are more..."

Ri latched onto Rozul's glove and yanked hard to shut him up. Rozul had bad bargaining instincts. They had the frog right where they wanted him, and Rozul wanted to give away their treasure!

The frog's eyeballs bugged out to a strained and painful distance. Nico stammered, "M...m...more?"

Ri cackled too loud. "He means, there are more ways to pay you." He snagged the shard from Nico's webbed grip. He tossed it upward like he was flipping a quarter. "You think this shard will cover it?"

The frog's yellow eyes glowed and caught fire. "Oh, yes. And then some. That is worth a fortune in my universe. I could sell it, pay off my equipment, and work only part-time. That would cover the gap in my retirement." A bit of drool slid down the frog's vocal sac.

He tossed it up, and Nico's whip tongue caught it. Ri grinned. "Then we're square."

The frog cradled the shard and fixated on its sleek ebony form. "Is there anything else I can do? I'm now in your debt."

The sun hovered over the horizon. His mother would come home any second to a destroyed house. "Yes! Please! Can you fix a doghouse and a living room? And my bed?"

"Huh. You gonna challenge me, little meatball? I pieced together the 150 quadrillion lines of DNA code fragments making up our quark star here. Another five minutes and your mentor would've blown this universe to smithereens."

Ri frowned. "Less talking, more doing."

"Right. Got it. On it." Nico used a couple robotic arms no more complicated than a house vacuum. With quick lightspeed movements, Nico repaired down to the last splinter every broken piece of evidence. The house sparkled along with Rozul's repaired body.

The house shined so much he feared his mother might suspect something. He analyzed the neighborhood through his bedroom window. The black hole heads continued to stroll, drive, and pass by. They paid no mind to the alien stunts happening in his house. In a few days, the world had flipped upside down. A universal agent pulling up in a spaceship and blowing a hole through his living room? The entire block should've erupted in panic! Not anymore. The adults in his world no longer cared. They had no heads to care with.

The frog tapped him on his shoulder with a long electric tongue. "Nanoseconds. I'm gone. Unless you wanna get a volcano at a waterhole. Kind of curious about this backwater 'verse."

Ri extended his hand for a shake—the bugged-eye response communicated volumes. The frog pushed his outstretched hand away. "No. No. This way." Nico lifted his webbed hand high.

Ri slapped his palm. "High five."

"What? No. High four. Duh, are you a meathead mammal? Oh yeah, that's right, you are. Okay. Nice doing business. Call me never again." The frog clapped his webbed digits. He jumped onto his gold-plated metal disk and surfed through the reopened wormhole. The frog shouted something else, but Ri couldn't hear it over the vibrating wormhole's roar.

The frog disappeared, and his bedroom returned to normal. The front door clicked closed. Ri's mom was home. Looking frantically at Rozul, he clamped his lips shut and placed a finger over them. He pointed at the closet. Rozul jumped up—featherlight—still lumbering, though traveling with a new kick in his step. He snuck into the closet the same moment Ri jumped into bed. With no time to shed his street clothes, he yanked the covers up.

This time, his mother didn't open the door. The door vibrated and the doorknob shook. Black tree tentacles crunched through the bottom of the door and crawled along the floor, like half a dozen blind snakes groping in the darkness. Ri swallowed hard and lay in the bed paralyzed. His mom was getting worse. So much worse. No longer human at all. The crack in the moon and their universe continued to unravel humanity. The tree tentacles climbed up the side of his bed and sniffed the air. They seemed to hear his heart pounding against his ribcage.

After five agonizing minutes, the tree tentacles retreated. The light in the hallway shut off.

Ri's body shook. He had to fix his mom. Time was running out. Would he be able to reverse this? Now that Rozul was fixed, they needed to create a solid plan. Find his sister and fix everything once and for all. *You're gonna get better, Mom. I promise.*

He tried to force himself to sleep. His anxious rumination kept him awake. The sheep nuzzled his face, taunted him with a deck of cards, a box of rolled clovers, and a bottle of fermented H2O. He squinted his eyes closed tighter. *Go jump over your stupid gate, you stupid sheep.*

They baaed at him with scorn and stepped over the crushed splinters of the gate. They kicked the pieces into the rushing river with their back hooves. Sticking out their tongues at him, they resumed their game of Go Fish.

He slipped into sleep, but accidentally into the worst kind of slumber.

26

The Whimsical World

THE MOMENT RI OPENED his eyes, he detected the wrongness of his world. A striking difference in the stickers on the ceiling above his bed glared at him. They appeared new; none of them were curling or peeling. And his Solar System included Pluto. Why would that interloper dwarf dare inhabit his ceiling? He pinched himself hard to determine whether he remained in slumber.

Shoving his hands under his pillow, he sniffed the air. He tasted staples and mozzarella cheese. Who contaminated his atmosphere? The thickness collected on his tongue—he sniffed in air globules of burnt grease. Something pounced on his chest, and he almost jumped out of bed. At first, he imagined an attack by one of Belez's devil rats, but the purring calmed his nerves. A Calico cat shoved its cold, slimy nose into his scowl.

Ri pushed the cat away. "What? We don't own a cat..." His heart skipped a beat. A note on the ground near his bedroom door shifted from a breeze. He whipped the covers off, knocking the cat off the bed—she hissed at him. Bouncing from the bed, he landed near the door and scooped up the note.

Dear Rieden,

We need to talk after school. Even if you wake up late, please go anyway. I've already called your teacher to tell him you'll be late. I'm taking off from work early tonight. I'm not upset with you. Please. Don't make this hard on us. See you tonight.

Love, Mom

Ri squinted at the note, reading it three times. He glanced up at the closet, a cold chill running down his arms. "Rozul! Rozul!"

The closet door whipped open. Rozul peered at him with a tilted head. "What's the matter? Have you eaten a ghost?"

Ri scrutinized the cat with suspicion and clutched the note tightly to his chest. "Something's wrong. I can feel it. Something crooked, something off. I...well...not sure...hey...what's the time?"

An Einstein cuckoo clock on the wall above his bed erupted. The tongue stuck out, and a horrific grinding vomited from Einstein's ironic mouth. Nine a.m. He gaped at the clock, and his legs melted into jelly. "That's *definitely* not my—"

Somebody pounded on his window. He jumped and dropped the note. Nobody knocked on his window...except, except. The memory connection eluded him.

The window slid up and open from the outside. "Rieden Reece! What monkey business are you up to?"

The shock smacked him in the face. Shelly Sanderson. At his bedroom window. What? Why? How?

Shelly grinned. "Cat got your tongue?" She giggled and gestured at the angry cat licking her front paw while snubbing Ri.

He pulled his jaw up tight. "Er. Shelly. Hey. How, um, may I help you?"

Shelly tilted her head sideways, her long, dark curls dancing. "What? Come on! We're late for school! No way you're ditching again; you'll lose attendance points, and my boyfriend's not going to fail this year!"

When she uttered "boyfriend," he staggered backward from the emotional punch to his gut. His eyelids fluttered thirteen times, and he gawked through psychedelic layers of shock. Her cheeks sparkled with a pink, candy sheen. The curiosity of her cheeks overcame his horror at her words.

She put one hand on her hip and with the other, she clutched the window frame until her knuckles turned bone white. "Ri! Are you listening to me? Why are you staring? Get dressed. Lose those ridiculous pajamas and move."

He shuffled around his bed. He passed a frozen Rozul—his glove over his mouth—and approached the scary girl. She glared at him with controlling eyes. The sunlight exposed a clear image. Every inch of her skin reflected the shiny shimmer of cotton candy.

No way he'd touch her again.

Shelly stretched out her hand and caressed his chin. The soft, sugary fibers tickled his skin. She jammed her pink eyebrows together. "What is it, darling? Are you running a fever?"

His instincts executed an instant plan. A way out. He fake coughed with forceful intention. "Yes. Totally sick. Delirious. What day is it? Who are you? Um, I"—fake yawn—"can't stay awake...."

Shelly crinkled a deep frown. "What? Your mom called mine and said you were going to school today. The teacher let me come get you."

Now he *knew* beyond any doubt he was in the wrong universe. Teachers allowing students to run around, unattended? Ha! He grinned with ruthless intention. "I told my mom I felt better. I lied. She worries nonstop, of course. Gonna sleep all day and recover before she gets home."

Shelly pursed her lips and batted her big brown eyes at him. "Oh. Okay. I get it. Okay, baby doll, feel better." She lifted a superhero sticker book and handed it to him. "Here's your present. Oh, I'll miss you. See you tomorrow." She pushed her head forward as if expecting a hug, or worse, the dreaded kiss.

Ri coughed loud and hard. "Um, you'd better leave before you catch my cold too." He pushed her cotton candy hands clear of the windowsill and slammed the window shut. He waved at her, smiled stupidly, and closed the curtains. When he tossed the sticker book on his bed, sugar crystals sparkled in the sunlight.

Rozul unfroze. "Boyfriend? Did you and Shelly enter a contractual mating ritual while I waited in the closet?"

Ri jammed his palms into his eye sockets and rubbed violently. He growled, "Dude! No! Gross! Sick! Ugh! Don't you get it? We've slipped into the *wrong* universe!"

Rozul's colorful eyes exploded. He fumbled for his straw hat. He flipped it off and adjusted a three-dimensional image with his glove. "No. According to my coordinates, we continue to occupy the correct location."

"Your calculations are wrong! Figure it out, Shadow Man! I slept us into a bonkers universe. The cat, the clock, the Shelly." He stuck his tongue out like it was a hairball lodged in his throat. The cat paused in licking her paw and scowled at Ri.

Rozul flipped up a gloved finger. "Ah. Clarity. Alternate reality. Not universe. Our location is the same; your consciousness has simply slipped frequencies. You're observing an alternate reality."

Ri clutched a wad of his head hair and squeezed. "Calling it something else doesn't matter. Different universe, or different reality. We're not where we should be."

"I did warn you to stay cautious during your sleep cycle."

Ri pointed a shaking index finger. "Don't put this on me. You said be careful. You never mentioned how to avoid it. How do I sleep us back?"

Rozul fiddled with some more images scrolling above his straw hat. He waved his glove around with the grace of a drunk magician with Alzheimer's. He put his hat back on and grinned a scary clown's grin. "I've calibrated the coordinates. 55 percent chance I'll maneuver us back to your original reality. Or destroy the universe. Hmm, the correction cannot occur until your natural sleep cycle begins again tonight. Chemicals in your body, certain frequencies, and whatnot."

Ri's expression crinkled. "What? I've gotta spend an entire day in a universe where...where...." Her name tasted foul on his tongue. "You-know-who is my, my..."

Rozul kicked up a painted eyebrow and crossed his stick arms. "Shelly is your mate?"

Ri stumbled backward. "Did you not see her? Her entire body is sugar! Cotton candy! In what kind of messed-up universe does that happen?"

"Reality."

"Whatever! Ugh! I'm fed up with this stupid adventure. This twisted universe is out to get me!"

"Well. Someone woke up on the wrong side of the—"

"Don't finish that!" Ri stomped over to his closet and searched for some clothes. He discarded dozens of cringeworthy shirts on the floor and yelled, "We gotta track down more shards. Are there even shards in this universe? And grab my bike. I figured we could use a shard to reach through and snatch it in a flash. Fat chance. I gave up my only shard to save your life. And *you* tried to give him *more*! Now that we know they're a valuable commodity, we need to collect more. Use them for bargaining chips with the universal agent, the rat-cyborg, or the librarian. Who can possibly guess what might happen in this universe? Reality. Whatever."

He slipped on jeans and an ugly lime t-shirt. The shirt displayed a picture of Mt. Rushmore replaced with Newton, Einstein, Darwin, and Tesla. "This version of me needs to get a life." He flung his backpack over his shoulder.

"Where are we going?"

Ri growled, "Aren't you listening? We need more shards!"

Rozul placed a slow, deliberate glove against his chin. He swirled the painted colors with his forefinger. "Hmm. If you've translated shards into monetary value, that's an unwise priority. Money first is never a good goal. Since Nico fixed my body, I can track the location of gaps in my memory. We should fill those gaps first to find my sister."

Ri yanked open his bedroom door. "Come on. We can argue on the way. I'm afraid to guess what this universe is gonna throw at us. The shards have saved us more than once. It's not money to me—they're broken moon pieces with your star power mixed in. They are the keys to unlock doors. They will help us find the mystery boy and your sister." He stormed toward the front door.

Ri ignored the unfamiliar furniture. He ignored the odd knickknacks. He ignored the excessive number of irritating pictures scattered everywhere. The cat meowed at him to feed her. He ignored her, too, and swung the door wide open.

He immediately regretted that decision.

This reality crawled under his skin. Thousands upon thousands of shard clouds hovered above his town. The dense pockets drowned out the sunlight. Rivers of lava cracked the ground and ran precariously down the asphalt. The black hole heads had transformed. Their heads were doubled in size, and liquid chocolate poured out of them. Their human bodies were replaced with flowing chocolate. White chocolate. Dark chocolate. Milk chocolate. Some of the black hole heads flowed liquid rainbow candy. A few bodies flowed whipped cream with candy corn and marshmallows surfing down. The air smelled and tasted of bonfire ash mixed with burnt peanut butter. A couple of kids played jump rope in Fenway Park across the street. Their carved, melted chocolate bodies splashed through milk puddles.

A frigid wind chilled him to the bone. A flurry of snow brushed his cheeks. He stretched out his palm and caught a falling flake. It remained intact without melting. He examined it, sniffed it, and popped it into his mouth. Sugar flakes.

Rozul lumbered behind and knocked into him. "What? What is it?"

Ri grunted, "Life's not fair."

27

The Xenophobic Xerox

ROZUL AND RI SHUFFLED in silence. They jumped over lava river rapids to avoid burning into human toast. Ri collected dozens of low-hanging shards dangling in the sky, which were now nothing more than common overgrown weeds. He grew weary of them. Hiking on foot through this dangerous landscape took forever. It added up to less than zero sense.

He held on tight to one of the shards. That meant he could slice through the universe and retrieve his bike with ease. But his emotions bubbled in a cauldron of burning jet fuel. He had overslept and woken up in the wrong reality. He no longer trusted his ability to rip through space.

Rozul initiated several attempts to strike up a conversation about their next plan. Ri ignored him until he fell silent.

An hour later, they reached the dilapidated old museum. An extra sticky humidity permeated the air. The old machinery lay defeated and covered with a hot morning dew. The rust formed liquid gold and dripped into shimmering pools. Ri almost reached out to touch a golden puddle. It appeared toxic, though. He located his bike right where he'd left it, tucked in between an old tractor and a rusted trailer. The viscous alternate reality dew drenched his bike.

He searched for something he could use to wipe down his bike. Parading into the nearby shed, he found a dirty oil rag in the never-emptied, rusted trash can. He wiped off the dew without much success, smearing most of it. The rag failed to absorb much, and the golden moisture coagulated into gelatin. He did manage to dry his seat.

He started to walk his bike along the museum grounds, but Rozul blocked his exit. Rozul stood tall, holding his painted head high, his straw hat dancing in the breeze. He crossed both his wooden arms and glared, his two painted eyebrows pushing down his eyes. "You must lend me your deaf ears. I have something important to tell you."

Ri frowned. "What?"

"I have received a communication from my sister."

Ri's jaw dropped open, and he almost let go of his bike. He gripped the handlebars, and his thoughts spun out of control. His foul mood evaporated. "What? When did this happen? Why didn't you tell me sooner?"

"I tried many times. Your insulting face blocked me."

Ri shook his head. "Okay. Okay. I'm sorry. It's. Well. You know. Anyway. I'm sorry. Yes, yes. This is great news. Our first good break. What did she say? Where is she? Does she need us to do something?"

"It came via a weak broadcast. It sounded like she went to great trouble to get a signal to me. It was encoded; only I could understand it. It's more emotion than anything. But we need to get to a different location here on Earth so I can attempt to establish stable contact. The destination is specific. Based on what I received, I calculated she is in your solar system. I'm guessing she is glowing at the outer edge hiding near a dwarf planet."

Ri formed a fist and punched the air. "Yes. Is she safe? Did she outrun the evil that chased her into our universe?"

"She provided none of that information." Rozul adjusted his hat. "We must travel to the other side of town where I can send her a clear signal."

Ri bubbled over with excitement. Their new clear plan pumped energy into his veins. "This is great. We go find your sister. With your combined power, she can help you stitch the moon back together and fix the crack in our universe. That will fix my mom and all the black hole heads. Once everything is fixed, that should get the universal agent and the Librarian of Death off our backs. There's only one thing I still don't understand. What did the mystery boy in those leech memories have to do with us? That still isn't clear. Though my gut feeling tells me he's the key to putting this all together."

The wind picked up and blew at Rozul's hat. He slammed a glove hard against it, keeping it on tight. "Those memories of the evil one whose name I shall not mention were not ours. It painted the town a red herring color."

Ri shook his head and frowned. "I don't think so. It's all connected. You found the book. Those memories meant something. I can still feel I'm missing something, missing memories. My mind is still off. They weren't for nothing. Still. It's okay. We may not understand how it all fits together yet, but we're on the right track. We've found your sister! This is huge. I admit, Shadows, this alternate reality nonsense got to me. For a second, I thought we were gonna lose. And I can't lose my...." Ri stopped before saying the word "mom" out loud. A heavy wave crashed and cascaded through his body. He sucked in a deep breath and forced himself to regain his calm. "Come on. Lead the way. Let's go chat with your sister."

He swung his backpack across his shoulders the correct way and jumped on his bike. He pedaled off the museum grounds. Rozul lumbered beside him, leading the way. Ri traveled with fierce intention.

Regardless of how fast he pedaled, Rozul kept pace in a nonchalant, whimsical way. The moment he opened his mouth to speak, a weird wind blew bad tidings.

"What was that?"

"Wind."

Ri whipped his head from side to side as if Shelly had snuck up on him. "Duh, it's wind, Mr. State the Painfully Obvious. It's a peculiar wind."

"We're in an alternate reality. That's normal wind here."

Ri pedaled down a wide, nonpaved residential street. The old rundown houses lay spread out. Only a few lava rivers ran along this side of town. The wind howled with the intensity of monsoons kicking up a dark, dusty wall. The small half-moon faded in the daylight sky, chunks falling like a dry cookie crumbling. He pointed. "Wow. In this reality, you did a number on the moon. Smashed it to bits."

Just as Rozul gazed upward, the universal agent's spaceship burst into view. It arrived from nowhere and sizzled into space.

Ri slammed on his brakes and skidded. This agent's spaceship loomed three times bigger than the one from his home reality. The agent's suit arrived with an upgrade. The agent flew from the part of the ship where flames cascaded hot liquid magma. Their boots propelled them along by shooting out rows of azure beams. They headed straight for Ri and Rozul.

He reached for the shard in his pocket. It wasn't there. *Idiot!* He had stuffed them all into his backpack, and it would take too much time to stop and retrieve them. The agent would overtake him in seconds. Outrunning the agent came first. Ri slammed a pedal down, kicking up dust. Adrenaline surged through his body. He aimed for the front yard of the nearest house, hoping to dodge the agent.

An explosion hit the front of the house. The wind blast knocked him against his left side and almost off the bike. He spun it in the opposite direction and dove to the edge, where fewer flames ignited.

"That stupid agent is gonna get someone innocent killed!" he shouted. "I'll grab a new shard along the way. Or zoom far enough ahead to gain time to pull out a shard."

He dove along the right side of the house and surveyed all the way down to the bottom of the second-story porch. He darted his head sideways. "Did you hear me?"

Rozul no longer lumbered beside him. His telepathic voice shouted, *"Slow down!"*

Ri calculated the distance between himself and the agent's ship. The agent sped along with its turbo boots, gaining on Rozul. Ri searched below him for a good spot to whip around. His bike soared higher and higher and higher.

How did that happen?

No time to speculate. He flipped the bike around, and it performed an instant 180-degree turn, jerking his body and neck at an odd angle. Speeding forward, somehow his bike moved much faster than it should. The burning house lay beneath him—the flames broiled his feet.

Rozul waved frantically as the agent gained on him. Ri skidded sideways, sending wave ripples through the turbulent wind. He faced down, his heart beating fast. He dangled over nothing and ignored the crawling bug sensation consuming his limbs. Dealing with heights lodged a poisonous throbbing in this throat. He choked down the lump and shouted, "Rozul! Shrink! I'll grab you!"

Ri dove straight down at a 90-degree angle with his nose aimed at the ground. The agent approached in slow motion. Seconds later, falling at an incalculable speed, he swooped in on a shrinking Rozul. Rozul dwindled to half his size—not quite small enough. Ri snatched Rozul's shrinking glove. He flung his handlebars backward and pulled hard. He turned on a dime—the agent's boot flames slammed against his back tires. He pushed forward too fast. The bike rocket-launched, and he almost lost his grip on the handlebars.

Rozul dangled, a tiny flapping kite the size of a small toy. Ri soared up high at an impossible angle, a dozen feet off the ground. He almost crashed into the burning building. The agent fired another burning missile at him. It sailed past his cheek and hit the last standing part of the house. He choked on the smoke and lost visibility. Aiming up high, he lunged his body forward, propelling his bike along.

Rozul wrapped himself around the handlebars and hugged them tightly. The wind thrashed him; he looked like a flapping rag. The roaring of the agent's boots vibrated the bike—Ri avoided the risk of sneaking a glance.

Rozul whispered in his mind, *"How are you doing this?"*

Ri forgot how to speak with telepathy in that moment, so he shouted in panting rips, "Dunno. You. Me. This crazy reality. No time to analyze, gotta save our lives. I'm heading to the nearest patch of shards. Unless you can climb into my bag."

A series of exploding blasts knocked them into a dangerous spin. He twisted—a broken leaf in a tornado—and scrambled to regain his bearings. Flying high above a row of houses, he oriented himself over the familiar neighborhood. He tested the balance of his bike. The coagulated golden dew solidified as droplet streaks across his bicycle. It formed sleek ridges along every edge of the bike's metal frame. He slipped his hands across the grips. Achieving complete command over his motorcycle's antigrav thrusters came in an instant.

He tested the sensors on the handlebars and manipulated the video game-type controls. The bike tracked his hand and finger movements. One side grip ignited a blast of heat from the rear of his seat and shot him forward. "Whoa—cool!" He held on with a death grip, preparing for imminent battle.

The agent chased him from below, shooting their weapon nonstop. Atop his bike, Ri tumbled into a barrel roll, heading toward the street with the new houses and denser buildings. He aimed for the narrow alley nestled behind the houses. The obstacle course came lined with dumpsters, carport coverings, and wooden fences. He dove down there. He hoped he would gain enough distance ahead of the agent to grab a shard and portal jump.

Rozul slipped off the handlebars. Ri's ninja reflexes snagged him. He pulled the tiny alien in tight and situated him on the top tube. "Rozul, use your powers. I'm buying us time. You've got this. How many times have we escaped the universal agent? Work your star power!"

"I'm faltering to think with all this commotion. I'm used to having centuries to make decisions."

Ri clenched his jaw. *Useless.* Oh, yeah, Rozul could read his thoughts. Oh well, Rozul would thank him after he saved their lives. How fast could his upgraded anti-grav bike travel?

Only one way to find out. He leaned forward with a wicked grin. "Hold on!" He pushed the handlebar controls down and ignited all the thrusters simultaneously. Unable to track his speed, he guessed he was traveling at 200 miles per hour.

The tempest blew through his hair, and pockets of air razors sliced up his body. "Dude! This version of the agent comes amped up on crazy juice!"

"I've been reading its motivation. It harbors an intense hatred for aliens."

"Duh, Mr. Obvious!" Another blast from the agent's weapon almost disintegrated his bike. Pivoting sideways, he flipped into a rough spin. He recovered, dove at a tilted 45-degree angle, and slid down into the alley. Now he was in his element. The obstacles whizzed by at impossible speeds. He flipped the anti-grav bike and traveled sideways along the wooden fences. His precognitive reflexes dodged trash cans, furniture, dogs, car parts, and random debris. The alley of death. A 3D video game he mastered.

The universal agent's silence caught up with him. "Did we lose our tail?"

Rozul's whipping limbs hugged the bike. *"I hear the agent's anger burning. Not tracking their location."*

That moment lasted forever. The alley spread open—Ri jammed his brakes hard, nanoseconds too late. The universal agent's weapon blasted the crossroad and spun his bike out of control. A molten scarlet lasso sizzled through the sky. The slithering snake wrapped around his body and reeled him in tight, squeezing the air from his lungs.

Darkness enveloped him.

28

The Zealous Zookeeper

R EALITY ARRIVED IN RIPS.

Consciousness. Something from the past. Or his future.

A newborn. An infant. A child. Why the unfamiliar thoughts?

The sensation of falling returned. Gravity tugged at Ri's internal organs. Dark, monstrous hands reached through his skin and clawed at his insides. He wondered if he was snoring away in his bed, suffering from a nightmare. Maybe this was just sleep paralysis giving him an adrenaline explosion.

He pushed through molasses to form words. "Mom. Mom. Can you hear me? I wanna wake up."

An echo whispered in the distance. Living words adrift through the cosmos, not tethered to a coherent timeline. "Oh. How sweet. The brat wants his mommy."

He recognized that voice. Those venom-filled words. The Librarian of Death. The Guardian Protector. The alien he hated more than canned lima beans. Her poisonous and contemptable words crawled deep into his ears. They chafed and filled him with murderous motives.

Or was something else pestering his ears?

Shooting pain rippled through his wrists. Bonds restrained him. Something—some intense power or force—bound his body. He dangled. He moved his right arm. And his left arm. Chains, or energy handcuffs. A force held him tight.

"It appears the little troublemaker is ready for spectators."

A snarl. "Good. Get this over with. I'm famished. Spending time and energy in this dump gives me an irritating itch. Smells of putrid peppermint."

Another familiar voice. The rat-cyborg. Ri licked his lips. The air in this place tasted like death. A foul rot. He forced an exhale, trying to speak again. He coughed. Staples and fishing wire held his mouth in place. No. No. No staples or wire, only pain. His mouth ached and tasted dry. "Water."

"Oh. The poor baby is thirsty. The dry meat requires hydration." Silence.

Another deep snarl. "What am I, room service?" A snap echoed. The prickling and crawling sensations spread along Ri's limbs. He forced open his lead eyelids. Darkness expanded into deep infinity. The clear outline of the librarian and the rat-cyborg shimmered. They occupied an odd position in space. Ri gazed through an eternity down at his floating body hanging on nothing.

Sewer rats crawled all over him.

His stomach flipped somersaults. He shut his mouth tight. A dirty straw dripped water into his mouth from a bundle of rats manipulating the source with their paws. The rot from their disease wafted—decaying meat from a crowded slaughterhouse.

Ri gagged.

Belez flexed a mighty bicep. "Yesss! What defeat! This is how you rewrite history. Simple building blocks of energy in this 'verse make it stupid simple. The great Rieden Reece. How the arrogant fall." Belez's hyena laugh echoed down the expanse of endless space. "Mad props to that universal agent we subcontracted. They tracked down our scared little animal and delivered on time. Packed a quick punch."

Ri craned his neck forward and stared down at his feet. He stood on nothing. And the empty void of space speckled with distant stars continued into infinity. To his left, planet Earth hung upon nothing. And the cracked moon sprayed the atmosphere with meteorite particles. He rolled his heavy head to the right. Full-sized Rozul hung upside down, his left leg bound by a glowing energy cuff. He dangled, suspended on nothing, the painted frown on his face flipped into an eerie upside-down smile.

Ri's soul groaned. He focused his mind, reminding himself how to use telepathy. *"Are you okay?"*

The librarian glowed, a sparkling star in the surreal ebony stage. She crossed her claws across her chest. "Oh. How touching. Feeble attempts to transmit to your mentally disturbed friend. He's a bit smarter than you, though, since he's, well, older than your solar system. He shut down his psyche. I can read all the electromagnetic energy on this shelf."

Ri shook his body. "Are the rats necessary? They keep tickling and scratching me."

Belez flexed his bicep and pointed with a razor nail stretching too far. "Your poison words are ineffective here, animal. We're calibrating. Soon, you'll answer to the Mirror of Truth."

The librarian adjusted her spectacles with her furry claws. Her snake tongue snapped out, sending a spark into the darkness. "This is satisfying. Should we torture him now? Start with physical and then psychological? Or reverse? Or start staggering the order randomly? I want all the torture, now!" She expanded her claws, and the tiny rats crawling all over him tugged on his energy cuffs. Surges of electricity shocked him into spasms.

Ri shouted and collapsed into a pathetic whimper.

The librarian slipped into her condescending pacing. With the lack of direct sunlight in this place—wherever here existed—she strode with a semi-normal gait. She placed her paws behind her back and puffed out her haughty chest. "You. The disappointing part with capturing you so young is your utter lack of awareness of what you've lost. So, I will enlighten you first, so you can mull it over and digest the defeat. Then back to the torture. It'll taste so much better."

The librarian reached into a dark pocket of space near her and pulled out Ri's backpack. A laser shot from her index razor finger and sliced a slit down the side. She dumped the contents into floating space, and they hovered. "Eh? What do I spy with my evil eye? A collection of useless rocks?" She retrieved a large shard. She waved it in a random pattern like using a piece of chalk to scribble rubbish onto a chalkboard.

She sneered. Her sharp teeth reflected glints of moonlight. "Aw. A wee bit of juice. It can cut through the fabric of space and time. How cute. Not even clever. The Protector's botched energy transfer. It fused potential energy and synthesized with these pathetic pieces of moon rock. Too bad channeling star memories into an infinite universe is a disastrous idea."

She shooed away the floating shards—soap bubbles popping in her face. She removed the black book from his backpack. A scorn-filled scrutiny surfaced from behind her spectacles. "Now this. This, I admit, is clever. What to call this from your limited, human perspective? A cache? A thumb-stick? Oh, let's see. Oh, yes, a backup hard drive. A well-thought-out plan by the Protector. Shove the body through. Download memories here. In case the consciousness gets compromised, back it up. Yes, quite clever. Safe. Too bad it failed to work the way the

Protector envisioned it. That often happens. Existence. It's got a wicked sense of humor."

Belez sighed.

The librarian cocked her head sideways and glared down her spectacles at the rat-cyborg. The direction her gaze traveled hinted that they existed in different physical spaces. "You want to contribute?"

Belez put his claws up behind his ears and floated in space with his matted furry feet extended. "I'm exhausted from all this talk. You rule followers are all the same. Why wait for the Mirror? Let's kill 'em and collect the bounty. I've got better things to do than wait around for some bureaucrat on a power trip enforcing arbitrary rules."

The librarian motioned with her paw, and another shock sent Ri into spasms. His scream melted into a whimper and petered out. He bit his tongue.

The librarian's penetrating fusion reactor eyes glowed. "That's a vote for more torture?"

Belez snorted. "Trivial. Wake me up when this is over. Torturing animals is too juvenile for me."

The librarian's claw waved a wide circle, gesturing into the inky void. "I prefer psychological warfare. Watch and learn what dusty archaic rules can do to a young soul." She rubbed her razor claws together. The friction sent lightning bolts around the circumference of a dark ball of energy. Inside the energy shield encasing, a small light burned bright. Its glow sent calm waves through Ri's every nerve ending.

Rozul, for the first time since he awoke, gasped. His painted face glowed hot and waves of joy rippled outward, with the calming energy from a vast sea. "My sister!"

Ri followed Rozul's gaze back to the light burning within the ball of the energy. That's *his sister*? He snapped his eyebrows together. The

Librarian of Death equaled the same evil who'd kidnapped Rozul's twin sister. "Let her go! She's not yours to steal!"

The librarian flicked out her snake tongue. "Ah, yes. Sending you two a fake signal to lure your movements out into the open. Simple traps for simple minds." She bared her shark teeth.

Dangling upside down, Rozul shivered. "You're no Guardian Inspector!" he shouted so loud that Ri's skull vibrated. "You're an imposter! I will expose your arrogant lies to the Mirror!"

The evil librarian laughed maniacally. Her voice resonated at the same treble of razor nails scratching a chalkboard. "Delightful! Tell me another one, you funny clown, you!"

29

The Judicial Juxtaposition

THE EVIL LIBRARIAN TOSSED the miniaturized star sister into space. The small star lodged in an unseen web of energy. The spherical prison glowed with a faint small flicker—a tiny light in a dark room. The librarian pointed up. "Ah, memories. You remember this one, Belez?"

A three-dimensional scene erupted to life. The texture and feel reminded Ri of the memories he'd extracted from the black book. A new memory. Belez and the same mysterious boy conducted some sort of business transaction. Crates of equipment loading and unloading from one spaceship into another. The crates rested upon small mossy blobs, changing shape and sliding with unexpected speed. The slugs slithered along and expanded. They shoved the heavy glowing crates inside the spaceship. Belez and the mystery boy spoke with inaudible dialogue.

The librarian paused the playback. "Perplexed, eh? Oh, what's this?"

She waved her claws to the opposite side. A radiant spotlight lit up another dark corner of space. A small, dome-shaped cage filled with a clear liquid appeared. A small human boy faced away from them, with energy cuffs binding his wrists behind his back. Ri could only see his short brown hair and light skin. The boy's familiar energy matched the profile from the image on the screen.

This was the same boy with downloaded memories he'd hitched a mental ride along with. The mystery boy who knew him somewhere in the future. Knew him well enough to visit his tombstone. Ri's curiosity for the mystery boy's role in this perplexing puzzle tugged at his heart. Somehow, this boy was the key. He knew it.

The rats chewed on his skin and dug in their claws deep. He winced and whimpered. "Ugh! I'm so sick of you—you stupid, idiotic, pathetic, worthless piece of garbage! Leave us alone! Give Rozul his sister back. Let that poor human boy go, whoever he is. Go to some other universe and pick on someone your own size!"

The librarian giggled and rubbed her chin with her razor nails. "My, my, my. How quickly they break. Weak, weak energy. Spinning around, getting nowhere. It's amazing your future adult self wreaks so much havoc through this universe. What's that basic Earth expression? A mustard grain. Seed. Same thing. Something so tiny becomes great. Explains why I'm here. To prune this sprouting little intellect. Squash it before it recognizes its power. Crushing souls, taking power, ruining lives. Oh, wow, it's so delectable. Delightful? Decadent? Ah, yes. Yes! Nice! Begging for mercy and accusing me of being a bully, yet you fail to yield to the truth. Your twisted brain bent and broken, like a crushed toy beyond repair."

Belez grunted. "Finally. Enough of this babbling claptrap. The Mirror of Truth is in sync. Will you shut up now?"

The librarian's eyes blazed, and she backhanded Belez across the snout. Belez caught her wrist with his powerful grip before she made contact. He held it, staring her down. They pushed each other away. A dark, swirling cloud of gravity mixed with magnetism morphed in the space between them. A miniature black hole, sucking in the surrounding energy with deliberate determination. A circular swirl of dark energy and crushed matter flowed into the center. The imploding waves formed rounded ripples. A small, shimmering light radiated. It gleamed with flawless purity.

The Mirror of Truth.

The Mirror of Truth vibrated and hummed, sending out waves of rippling energy. Not a calm pulse like Rozul's sister star. And not the malevolent pounding like the librarian or Belez. The cosmic current communicated strength, justice, wisdom, and something else. A hint of compassion?

The central point of the Mirror churned a steel blue. A watchful eye. An all-seeing entity. It spoke, electromagnetic pulses traveling through the void of space by unfathomable tech. "Calibration complete," it said in a deep, rumbling, authoritative voice.

Ri shook away the rats and tried to concentrate on the Mirror's presence. Could he trust this alien entity? Would it see truth, or a twisted version of lies humans claimed represented truth?

The librarian crossed her paws behind her back. "We're ready to proceed."

The Mirror rumbled out rules: "Each entity will speak in turn. All will complete their testimony until my interpretation is clear. Then I will render judgment. Does the accused fathom why they are standing trial?"

The librarian waved a dismissive paw at Rozul. "He's hanging more than standing, but of course. He's older than this solar system. The Protector is quite cognizant of his indiscretions. Forty-two in total."

The Mirror's eye rotated, a powerful flashlight piercing Ri's soul. "And this young intellect, not of mature criminal age. Why is he present?"

The librarian cleared her throat. "Appearances are deceiving, oh great Mirror...."

"Deception is impossible. And the judge disregards flattery."

Ri fought the urge to snicker. The librarian was already struggling with her weak case. *Serves her right.*

She rolled her eyes and pushed her spectacles up. "Yes, of course. He's the coconspirator. He helped the Protector severely damage planet Earth. A planet far from reaching complete consciousness. A populous unable to process the chain of events the Protector caused. We're asking the court to consider the extraordinary circumstances and waive the child's rights. Genocide is murder, after all. We request this juvenile be prosecuted for adult crimes."

"State specifics. Who is we?"

Belez extended a bicep and flexed. "Me and her. We're suing the scumbag."

The Mirror's eye rippled and focused on Belez, an instant relocation. "Belezashan Blaze. Wanted for crimes in thirteen universes and thirty-nine jurisdictions. This is an unprecedented appearance. A criminal warlord of your stature doesn't risk high-profile exposure. You are forming an alliance with Janenti-kel Jee-hi-En. You are broadcasting a message."

The librarian adjusted her skirt and readjusted her spectacles. "I give no consent to the use of my legal name. Guardian Inspector will suffice for the court."

The Eye flipped and zoomed in on the librarian. "You are not a Guardian. You purchased your credentials illegally in the way station outpost 2691-KRN. You've been impersonating a Guardian in this universe because the sentient life here cannot enforce code."

Ha! Figures. Ri stifled a grin. He formed two fists and pulled against his chains. The Mirror was already exposing the truth. Maybe he wouldn't need to create an escape plan after all—if the Mirror could see through the piles of lies.

The librarian curled up her evil lip. "Semantics. What's legal in one 'verse is brilliant in another. You're bound by future law in this sector. Advanced future humans will keep their provision for prosecuting children for adult crimes. If the court analyzes the future history, you will conclude Rieden Reece is no ordinary human. He meddles in universal activity many decades before others of his pathetic race. He has a dangerous spirit. And questionable ethics."

The Mirror of Truth's calming azure flashed a hot crimson for a nanosecond. "Using loopholes after breaking a multitude of laws in a multitude of universes. And you pass judgment on ethics? There is a sharp contrast between the role you profess and the person you portray. You are a bold creature, Janet."

Ri snorted. The rats clawed at him, and he coughed.

The librarian wrinkled her forehead. "Please. I request the court to recognize my Guardian status and refer to me as such."

The Eye flashed. "You compel copious requests of the court. I am patient. Order of testimony, Guardian?"

The librarian shrugged with a whimsical wave of her hand. "Let's hear from some Protector testimony. He's been awfully silent. Choking on his litany of crimes, no doubt."

A beam of blue energy pulsated from the Mirror of Truth and shined a spotlight on the upside-down Rozul. Rozul's painted eyes fixated on his imprisoned sister. A sparkling tear dangled and dropped. It splashed with a resounding pop and echoed into the endless void of their spatial prison. Rozul's heavy sigh continued into a terrible moan. His eyes formed into jagged zigzags. He spoke with a soft whimper, "Separated for so long, and yet still light-years away. My burning heart grows cold."

Ri wanted to try and talk to Rozul with telepathy, but he was a bit worried it could cause problems. If the Mirror was on their side, he didn't want to do anything to disrupt the courtroom. Not yet anyway.

The Mirror hummed along undeterred. "Displays of emotions are stricken from the court. Proceed, accused criminal."

While the others focused on the Mirror, Ri aimed his attention at Rozul. Ri itched to use telepathy and encourage him: *Don't give up, Rozul! We've got this.* And then Rozul did something rather unexpected.

Rozul winked.

Ri forced himself not to react. He caught his jaw before it fell open and his eyes before they opened wide. Rozul had a plan after all. Ri whipped his head to the left to make sure the librarian hadn't spotted their exchange. Small problem. His head refused to move. His eyes, his jaw, and his entire body stayed locked in place. The entire courtroom, a paused channel. It took Ri a split-second and all of eternity to grasp the situation. But then the obvious answer locked into place.

Rozul had stopped time.

30

The Yoked Yellow

"*C*AN YOU HEAR US?*"

Ri unblinked his frozen eyelids. The floating-in-space courtroom stuck in the stopped shelf. The Mirror's beaming eye a solid glow trapped in time. He connected the cosmic dots. *"Dude. You stopped time!"*

"Speak with soft thoughts in your mind. The librarian surveils us with deep suspicion. She scrutinizes your micro-expressions with scrubbing tech. We cannot let her ascertain our capabilities. I do not retain the ability to stop time. I downloaded this memory into your brain; for a linear creature, it mimics the stopping of time."

"You come up with a plan for getting us outta here?"

"No. My sister did. She is channeling energy from your yellow star."

A gentle voice spoke. *"Hello, little spark. My brother has never shared our connection with another being. Thank you for being so kind to him during his search for me."*

Ri had acted the world-class jerk to Rozul the entire adventure. His mom always called him her prickly cactus. Only certain types of weirdos appreciated cacti. *"Sure. Yeah. Of course."*

Rozul's voice continued, *"I'm utilizing the communication pen I gave you. We're concealing this transmission with undetectable energy. One misstep and the Guardian Inspector can intercept our transmission. My sister is far away from her, though we are ready to sync. Syncing will produce the power to break the hold the Guardian has placed around her and return her atoms to our universe."*

Ri sucked in a deep breath—impossible without the flow of time. His awareness nested inside an instant memory. He'd grown so attached to Rozul it never occurred to him what might happen when Rozul found the better half of his whole. Of course. Ri didn't own Rozul; his star friend possessed free will and chose his own trajectory. He kicked up a nonchalant grin—again, impossible. *"Great. We win. Should I help?"*

"Yes. I'm unable to send you any more communication or updates on our status. Keep watch on the Guardian. You cannot let her discover what my sister and I are planning. No second chances here. Divert her attention. Do what you do best: use your number one superpower. Engage her in pointless b anter."

"Um. Okay. I guess. That's all?"

"That's everything. She cannot interrupt our concealed connection. Rile her up, upset her, make her so angry she can't think straight. You've mastered the art of arguing. Your gift. The point is, the more she focuses on you, the less chance she'll unveil our activities. Do you understand?"

Ri almost roared at Rozul for his implication. But he stopped himself. Rozul was right—he did love to argue with everyone concerning everything. He solidified his will. The resolve might have come from Rozul's calm and authoritative voice. Or it could've sprung from his own gumption to help. *"Okay. I won't let you down. If anyone can torque off the librarian, it's me!"*

The broken valve of time flipped open and exploded all over the courtroom. The librarian whipped her pivoting owl head and stared down Ri.

"Getting infected with rat-bite fever over here," he snapped. "Can somebody call CPS already?"

The Mirror of Truth's spotlight narrowed its beam. "No interruptions from the court during defense testimony."

Rozul continued to whimper and moan. He meandered at great length concerning his woe at being disconnected from his twin sister. The separation anxiety. The loneliness. The acceptance of his codependent relationship.

While Rozul babbled on with great theatrics, playing the victim card, Ri calculated and plotted. For some unknown reason, the Mirror of Truth never focused its eye on Rozul's sister or the mystery boy. The Mirror acted like they weren't even there. The physics of the courtroom were beyond Ri's understanding. Somehow, the librarian must have manipulated the tech constructing the courtroom. The librarian was hiding the fact she had abducted Rozul's sister from the Mirror. So many crimes.

The chains chafed Ri's wrists. He needed to come up with a plan B, in case Rozul's sister struggled to do her thing. Somehow, he needed to figure out how to get the Mirror to see the mystery boy in the cage. The mystery boy held precious secrets—he was sure of it.

Ri might have been swayed by Rozul's tale of woe had he not received his powerful mental message. The librarian glared at him. He rattled his cuffs. "Water. Water. Why hold a useless trial if I'm gonna die anyway from thirst?"

The Mirror of Truth flickered mercury light. "Interruptions."

Ri shrugged and chafed against a chained wrist. The rats crept along his skin, lifting the water straw to his mouth. He sucked the water loudly, and the slurping echoed across court-space. He finished and exaggerated his contentment. "Ahh. Yes. So good."

Belez flipped inappropriate finger symbols his way. The librarian stood up straight—stiff as a corpse—her claws clutched behind her body. She peered down at him through her spectacles, her eyes twin flames.

Rozul made it obvious he intended to speak at pathetic level ten. He exaggerated his tone as he cried, "And the quantum entanglement! I lost her. The evil, the evil trapped her. I couldn't control my compulsion. I couldn't help myself. I didn't meeean to break the world. This place is so small, and it was a tight fit. My butt is bigger than I remembered. I knocked the little moon an itsy teensy bit. How can I help it if it's so fragile? Why would a planet with sentient beings have a cheap vase for a satellite? Please, you must grok. The Guardian is the evil one!"

The librarian's pupils sparked, and her chest heaved. Rozul covered his painted features with his gloves. Globules of tears floated away and glimmered in the Mirror's electromagnetic spotlight.

The Mirror thundered with an uncompassionate question. "Are you quite finished?"

Rozul peeked a painted eager eye from between a gap in his glove. "Yes. Finished. Finished like the Mona Lisa."

The Mirror flipped an instant optic on Ri. The spotlight burned bright. "You may begin your testimony."

Ri stretched his aching limbs. His restraints pushed hard against him. He forced himself to stand upright from his slouching position. Extending his aching back, he reached out with trembling arms. "Wrongful imprisonment. Unlawful torture. Lying to the courtroom." He paused. "Um, Mirror of sacred Truth and bearer of burdensome knowledge, how long am I allowed to testify?"

The Mirror of Truth thundered, "However long the accused requires."

Ri grinned wickedly. "Excellent!"

31

The Unfair Universe

U NLIKE MOST OF HIS classmates, Ri loved giving speeches in front of the class. When all eyes focused on him, his mind buzzed with excitement. But now was different. Failure was not an option. He needed to speak with a conviction like never before. He needed to persuade the Mirror of Truth to let them go so they could save his universe. He decided to channel his English teacher's personality: Mr. Coldbell. Usually, when Ri channeled Mr. Coldbell it was to make fun of him. Not now. Not in this moment. He needed the personality of someone with fearless conviction—someone who wasn't afraid to make a fool of himself.

Mr. Coldbell often quoted Shakespeare and other boring dead people from the past. And his English teacher would misquote them on purpose to test the students. Shelly's hand would shoot up and correct him. Ri had zero interest in who said what, but he mixed and mimicked Mr. Coldbell's quotes to begin his speech. He cleared his throat and rattled his energy cuffs for emphasis. "Aliens of another universe, I perceive that in all things ye are too superstitious. Worshipping laws failing to represent absolute truth."

The Mirror of Truth strobed the spotlight. "We do not worship. We obey laws keeping interspecies conflict to the lowest statistical probability. This is not absolute truth."

Ri lifted an extended index finger and jabbed it hard into space. "Ah ha! Double ha! You admit, oh great Mirror of Truth, whose moniker implies an adherence to truth. You admit you do not follow truth! Lies. This court is full of lies!"

The Mirror's optic shutter flashed a shimmering alloy orange. "I'm built incapable of lies. State specific situations for the court. There are thousands of theories and beliefs regarding truth. I'm built to follow the three most widely purported truths in the dominant universes. One: perceived truth. This is a truth pertinent to an individual, group, or system. This truth may benefit those who believe it. Yet, it crumbles under scrutiny from outside subjective perception. Two: absolute truth. This type of truth withstands the rigor of various perceptions. It withstands testing and adheres to accepted physical laws. Three: unknown truth. This is a future truth, a truth we cannot yet perceive that may, in fact, unravel many or all absolute truths. I could extract hours explaining the nuances and ramifications of each level of truth. I'm not paid to lecture. I'm paid to pass judgment on criminals."

Ri scrunched up his eyebrows and pointed an accusatory finger. "Your inability to lie has given you away. You're doing this for money, sir! Bias! I *call bi-as* in the court."

A disturbance wave rippled from the Mirror's eye that approximated a fart. Ri shook a shackled fist. "Truth! I demand truth! The court is not treating me fairly! The judge admits he has taken bribes from the accusers!" He addressed an invisible audience watching from the inky void.

Belez pulled out a glowing sidearm and pointed it at Ri. He growled, saliva spitting through space, "I'm itching everywhere listening to this obnoxious kid ramble. I'm gonna end our misery and—"

The Mirror shook, and a deep, resonating rumble roared through the space-court. "Silence! Only the accused may speak now. No matter how irrelevant or damaging to his own case."

The Mirror's steel-blue eye zoomed in on Ri. "This is the answer to your accusation. The criminals followed procedure in hiring an unbiased third party to manage the arbitration. And all actions in all universes rely on some sort of monetary exchange and market system. I am an entity with an unblemished and untarnished record of impeccable justice. If you are going to accuse me, align your facts with absolute truth. Not wild fantasies."

Ri squinted and toned it down a bit. He avoided the librarian's eye contact, though he noted her heated focus. "Point, oh Mirror of Amazing and Brilliant Truth. I apologize for jumping to conclusions. Please hear me out. I stand before you, innocent of any crime these two claw-brains accuse me of. The charade is not even well cloaked. They intend to snuff me out before my adult self has a chance to make a mark on the universe. I assume there exist rules against such sort of time travel to undo a person's life. Especially when such life is one of making the universe a *better* place. Not because it gets in the way of *two known criminals'* future lawless and cutthroat activity."

The Mirror flashed molten metal. "Yes. If you implied the truth, then such time manipulation is criminal. Nevertheless, they accuse you of helping an interloper destroy your planet. I am bound by this accusation and compelled to honor the download of the law."

Ri dropped a frown and grumbled, "That's dumb. All they had to do was stop interfering with Rozul's plan. We've been working hard to fix the broken moon and the black hole heads. Rozul made a mistake. But we found information! We discovered the black book to fill in our gaps of memory. And the ugly librarian you call Janet is the one who illegally captured Rozul's twin sister! She's the criminal! Not us!"

The Mirror of Truth softened its plasma eye. "You can furnish proof of these activities?"

Ri creased his forehead at the librarian. A fierce fixation of her focus pierced him. She extended her arm, holding the captured star in her left claw. She sneered a devilish smile dripping with condescension. The vein in his forehead twitched—this visual transmission only visible to Ri. The librarian manipulated the space-court to taunt him.

He jerked his energy cuffs high and rattled them. "The truth! The truth is right there in front of you! Why can't you see it? Why can't you see the truth? You can't handle the truth! You're out of order. This entire court is out of order!"

A laser beam of energy particles rippled through the Mirror's spotlight and crumpled Ri to the smooth space floor. "Enough! Accusations! If you provide no proof, I am bound to the truth. That is universal law. Intelligent beings can accuse each other ad nauseam. The burden of evidence is necessary to maintain law and order. Do not mock my commitment and purpose of upholding sacred laws. The evidence of you and the Protector's crimes is obvious. A crumbling satellite. A ruptured space-time continuum altering the physical attributes of your planet. Can you provide proof to counter this claim? Otherwise, we will proceed to prosecute you both."

Ri failed to keep the Mirror's attention focused. He struggled to give Rozul and his sister more time. No matter what, he would never give up. He cleared his throat. "Yes. The crime suggests obvious, cut and dry. Permission to offer this scenario to the court. Let's postulate a person becomes a witness to a crime. That said person jumped into his car and chased down the perpetrator. And along the way, suppose the innocent witness 'accidentally'"—Ri tossed up the necessary air quotes—"runs over a house. Would you convict the innocent witness of a crime? Or would you give him a reward for tracking down the vicious criminal who kidnapped an innocent star? Rozul got carried away. He chased down the evil: the despicable, ugly, and ferocious Librarian of Death. This weak Janet, with pathetic claws and a sun allergy for losers, stole Rozul's life. He slammed into our moon by a slight miscalculation. He fixated on finding the disgusting and despicable Janet. It knocked out his memory so he couldn't immediately fix things. Trust me. He can fix this. He can patch up the moon, make it shine brand-new. He'll fix the black hole heads and any other alterations to our universe. You gotta give him a chance!"

The Mirror's eye softened, a gray mist burning hotter than the sun. The mist drifted down through the darkness. Ri had softened the Mirror's defenses. The Mirror's thunderous voice proclaimed, "First of all, horrendous analogy. *Yes*, the lunatic driver demands prosecution. Destruction of property and endangering those occupants. The correct action upon witnessing a crime is to contact the proper authorities. Let the trained personnel handle such situations. Second, Rozul is no innocent. He comprehends the universal laws. He should have never attempted to transfer his electromagnetic self into such a small, sluggish, behind-the-times universe. He did so without proper authorization and without the aid of trained personnel. Third, please refrain from insults and epithets in the court."

Ri shrugged. "Are you forbidding me from calling Janet a good-for-nothing, evil, disgusting, perverted, yucky, and smelly dirtbag?"

The Mirror closed its all-seeing eye. The Librarian of Death's claws squeezed tight and vibrated. Drops of blood dripped down her paws. Shimmering droplets broke free and floated through space.

Ri hurried to speak before the Mirror decided to cast its judgment. "Okay, oh Wise Mirror of Ancient Truths and Arbitrary Belief Systems. Yes. Am I permitted to call a witness?"

Electricity flowed in currents across the Mirror's ocular and sparked into the court. "Unfortunately. Yes. Is this an intelligence who observed the crime and offers supporting testimony?"

Ri shook an energy cuff at the mystery boy's back in the dome cage. The boy's shoulders slumped forward. When Ri mentioned him, his head cocked sideways, and his ears perked up. A dim light illuminated him to the bottom left of the Mirror's location. Floating particles of energy twinkled around the mystery boy.

Ri announced, "I call the mystery boy. A known associate of Belez, and we're somehow connected in the future. He's aware of how despicable, disgusting, and deplorable this smelly Janet is."

The Mirror of Truth beamed a bright light that heated Ri's flesh.

He covered his forehead and cringed. "Ahem. My bad. Did I use one of those epitomes again? Epitaph. Whatever."

32

The Kilowatt Kaboom

T HE MIRROR OF TRUTH radiated a spotlight from its central optic and examined the court. It flashed over Belez, Janet, and Rozul. "I do not observe this mystery witness."

Ri vibrated his energy cuffs at the dome cage. "Right there! Belez and Janet captured him to keep him quiet. He's the key! He's what I've been chasing."

The Mirror pulled back the spotlight, and its eye glowed. "Who is this mystery boy? What is his name? What information does he offer?"

Ri shook his head and shouted at the boy. "Hey! Boy, don't ignore me! Say something. Where are you? Where have you been? Why can't they see you? Help me! Help! Tell the court what you know and save us. Show them your iron will and burning brilliance."

The boy's ears perked up at Ri's rant. The mystery boy clutched the curves of the dome glass. He rotated his head. That proved a significant problem.

The mystery boy had no face.

He possessed smooth skin instead of eyes, nose, and a mouth. The sight of the faceless boy sent a crushing weight against Ri's chest. The mystery boy turned back around and slumped against his dome cage. He banged his head against the glass in a slow, desperate rhythm.

A lump caught in Ri's throat, preventing him from speaking.

The Mirror flashed computer digits across its eye. "Rieden Reece. Will you call a witness or not?"

Ri inhaled his breath, held it, and exaggerated his sigh. Tears welled up. This mystery boy moved across universes with strength, confidence, and unbeatable toughness. He savored those memories. The boy's power, his ability to manipulate, control, and conquer. And here he sat. Helpless, captured in a glass cage. With no face. No ability to see, speak, or help in any way. Ri choked down the defeat. All the fight burning in his bones melted into butter. Belez and the librarian would win. Rozul and Ri would rot in universal cages. Convicted of crimes so minor in comparison to the criminal warlords. It wasn't fair. It wasn't fair. *Life's not fair.*

The Mirror's ocular strobed energetic spheres of energy. "Well. Does the accused rest their case?"

Ri remembered Rozul and their plan. No matter what, keep the librarian distracted, focused on him. Falling into despair accomplished nothing. Though he believed the mystery boy would solve all his problems, he could only keep doing his part. Keep trying, until his dying breath. No giving up yet.

He lifted a cuffed wrist and waved his index finger. "And another thing!"

The librarian slapped her forehead with her paw, rattling her spectacles. "Let's end this brat's endless tirade of absolute absurdity, now!"

The Mirror vibrated. Before it could speak, Ri shouted, "Janet, you ignorant butt! The mystery boy can smell your putrid lies and he doesn't even have a nose! Go ahead and crawl back under the pile of dung you came from. No universe deserves you. A stupid, no good, ridiculous-dressing, four-eyed freak. You gluttonous book eater. Go take a long walk off a short pier, you poop-for-brains, rusty-nailed...."

The Librarian of Death failed to restrain her vibrating body. Before the Mirror could intervene, she screeched at the top of her lungs, "Kill that sack of meat!"

The small rats converged on Ri's body. They turned up the electric shock and sliced his skin with dozens of mini razor claws. He screamed—the convulsions reverberated through his limbs.

Belez leered. The Mirror of Death erupted, and rays of its pulsating energy gripped the librarian. She fell, her outstretched claw pointing—intensifying the torture. Ri's eyeballs swelled up, his hair electrified, and saliva drooled down his cheek.

The Mirror thundered, "Enough! You dare torture someone in my court!"

The librarian flailed in empty space, controlling the torture by virtual force. She glowed. Hotter and hotter. Sweat poured down her face and her spectacles fogged up. She formed a deep frown and peered down. The imprisoned star burned bright and seared Ri's retinas. Torture faded into the background. Overwhelming heat, light, and energy from Rozul's sister consumed the court.

The Mirror of Truth blasted an electron alarm. "This court has become a circus! Mistrial! And furthermore...." The bright shining star in the center enveloped the court. Ri shielded his eyes. The screams from the librarian reverberated, along with the sizzle of melting flesh.

The librarian disappeared. The rats ceased their torture. The invisible force holding Rozul upside down dropped him—he landed hard on the plane of empty space. Belez's eyes darted, and he clutched his weapon.

The Mirror of Truth rippled a flashing red alarm. "In all my billions of years, I never...."

Belez growled and spat. He whipped out his weapon and blasted the Mirror in the eye. Leaping through an invisible portal, he disappeared. The Mirror flickered and shined a spotlight on Rozul and Ri. A rumbling roared through itself, dark energy waves rippling inward. The swirling vortex consumed the eye—shrinking it smaller and smaller. It winked out of their dimension.

The mystery boy in the dome cage sat with his back to them. He lifted his left hand and gestured with two locked fingers. Ri had no idea what that meant. The mystery boy disappeared.

Rozul lumbered and tiptoed across empty space. He broke open the energy cuffs on Ri's wrists with his giant gloves. Ri collapsed. The torture reduced his limbs to jelly. He coughed out a jumble of mumbles, trying to say, "Did it work? Is it over?"

Rozul shushed him. "Grab on to my side. We leave now."

Ri flopped his jelly head toward the empty space-court and majestic Earth. "Where are we?"

"On a space shelf. Humans haven't learned how to manipulate dark matter. That includes the ridges of shelved circular space."

Rozul swam through empty space toward Earth, and Ri wondered aloud, "How can I breathe?"

"You're not breathing. This isn't the vacuum of space. Our imprisoned consciousnesses are waiting at the edge of the shelf. When we arrive there, I'll pull our bodies out of stasis. I'll protect you during the fall back into Earth's gravitational field."

Ri's implacable will to fight evaporated. Instead of disputing the plan, he mumbled, "Sounds dangerous. Won't you die?"

"Not at all. My sister helped me retrieve my memories from the black book. I remember what I did wrong. I've retrieved full access to my powers now. I conceive of what I need to do. Hold on. And hold your breath."

The sensation of gravity tugged at Ri's body in the wrong direction. He held on tight to Rozul as they flipped through space, plummeting out of control. The g-force crushed him, squeezing his bones inside out. He gripped Rozul harder and harder—the spinning made bile bubble up in his throat, and he almost threw up. The light from Earth, the broken moon, and the sun blinded him. He cranked his eyes shut tight, which intensified the motion.

Ri screamed.

Heat burned holes through his body. He processed the events in sharp snippets of awareness. Falling. Hot. Spinning. Speeding. Holding on. Losing grip. His hands falling against an unsurmountable g-force. His body flailing through space, a wet noodle in a hurricane. He screamed and screamed until his lungs emptied and flattened.

Rozul's telepathic voice whispered, *"Thanks for everything."*

Adrenaline pumped through Ri with alarming intensity. Yet, his molecular fiber trembled from a more powerful interruption. *Wait. What?* Rozul was leaving....

The gravity shifted and slammed into him. Rozul grew bigger and bigger, destined for the moon, his shadowed outline an arrow. He traveled at an arc, slamming his trajectory straight toward the moon.

The sky fell away—the earth rushed closer and closer. The wind tore at Ri's back, and he tumbled into a steady freefall. The sun dropped to his right and the moon above him. The moon shards sailed up the sky, converging on Rozul's enormous arc. Rozul—a blazing comet—accelerating and targeting the moon. Millions of speeding shards trailed from behind him.

The scene lasted forever on into all eternity. Ri fell, faster and faster. Flames cupped him during his acceleration down into Earth's atmosphere. An energy cocoon Rozul had formed around him controlled the heat. The ground came closer and closer. The moon shrank smaller and smaller, moving farther and farther away. Rozul—now thousands of miles away—closed in on the ancient orb.

Rozul slammed into the moon. Millions of shards collapsed backward, exploding inside out. Imploding. A spectacular fireworks display reeling itself inward. The detonation lit up the sky, and darkness enveloped the expanse. A sparkling rain of liquid mercury decorated the heavens.

Ri collapsed into the ground.

He struggled for breath and struggled to move. Stuck. Stuck in the ground. He ripped his right arm up and peeled himself away. As he heaved his body upward, heavy gravity weighed down his bones. He sat, leaning on the small boy-shaped crater. He blinked. He blinked again. Straining his noodle and neck, he gazed upward. The imagery enraptured him—an unfamiliar pale moon. Intact. Whole. Normal.

Where had he landed? He recognized Bess's doghouse. *Bess!* He occupied the correct reality. Slammed into his own backyard. *Rozul did it! He fixed the moon!* Ri had returned to the correct Earth reality.

The new insight invigorated him. He tore his aching body from the ground and brushed away the dirt and mud. He checked his rat bites. They faded. The pain faded. Rozul had fixed everything.

Would he ever see that crazy alien again?

A knot formed in his gut, and a lump caught in his throat. He choked back a tear. No matter. Sadness accomplished nothing. Rozul had found his sister. He'd fixed the broken universe. The tough voice inside him whispered: *Act happy for Rozul and avoid feeling sad he left. Missing him will accomplish nothing.* Ri had helped him. He'd helped him buy time so his sister could escape that stupid librarian's prison.

He grinned and sighed deeply.

A familiar voice he hadn't heard in a long, long time yelled at him, "What are you grinning about?"

His mom stood in the backyard near the house—arms folded and staring him down. Unbelievable! His mom's face! Her cranium sparkled whole, no longer a black hole. No more suffocating silence. "Mom! You're okay!"

She jammed a hand into her hip, hard. "Well, that makes one of us. You have a million things to explain and ten seconds to do it!"

33

The Nominal Normal

N O TIME AT ALL for Ri to savor his victory. Saving the world. Fixing the adults. Repairing the moon. None of it mattered now; he had to deal with the wrath of Mom.

He followed her into the house. She strutted in her "I'm serious" way, still wearing her navy-blue work scrubs. She held the door open for him, although she refused to make eye contact. His stomach churned and the bile burned his throat. This seemed like more than the usual lecture and grounding. The chill from his mother's stance stirred up a new unfamiliar dread.

He stepped onto the living room's carpet and slid to a stop. He did a double take and gaped. The Librarian of Death. Sitting in his living room. She was lounging in his mom's loveseat— holding a clipboard and beaming innocence. The librarian's gaze seared his emotional armor. She adjusted her spectacles with a gentle push of her human finger. His heart slammed into a frenetic beat. He gawked at the fabricated human. Wild conjectures of why she sat there slithered between his ears.

His mom's voice pierced his distracted attention. "Rieden. You remember Janet, the school counselor. She's come here to check up on us."

Ri stuttered, "School counselor? You mean librarian."

The normal human librarian, hiding her alien attributes, beamed. "Oh, yes. I do volunteer at the public library on occasion. I've seen you there. Always in the Science Fiction section, correct?"

He backed away from her with one cautious step after another. Any second, she might reveal her claws and slash his mom to pieces.

His mom approached him from behind and placed a firm two-handed grip on his shoulders. She faked a laugh. "Rieden loves to read. That's what they... He's always been an avid reader." She coughed and cleared her throat.

The crunching of gravel from car tires on their driveway drifted inside. Blue and red lights flickered from the kitchen, reflecting off metal surfaces. He twisted around and focused on the entrance. A female police officer marched up their steps and greeted them with a tip of her hat. Her strong vanilla perfume wafted into the house. The officer grimaced, placed her hands on her hips, and glared at Ri. He narrowed his eyes, unsure of why a cop would come to his house. A vague recollection surfaced of Brian mentioning a cop talking to his teacher. Would they arrest him for assaulting and stalking Shelly?

Well, at least he no longer existed in the universe where that crazy cotton candy freak claimed him as her boyfriend.

His mom lifted one hand from Ri's shoulder and gestured. "You remember my friend, Makena? I met her at the hospital several years ago. We've invited her over a few times to watch movies with us."

Ri's mouth fell open to speak. His mom's inflections trembled—one false move and he might increase his trouble exponentially. He faked a broad and ridiculous grin. "Um. Yes. Makena," he lied. "Movie night, sure. You look different in the uniform."

His mom squeezed his left shoulder hard. He'd already taken a misstep. She spoke through gritted teeth. "That's funny you don't recognize her. She's been chasing you all around town. Near canals and groves. Down alleys. In bars. She even picked you up once and brought you and your stuff here."

Ri's eyes flitted from Makena to his mom nervously. When Rozul had fixed the universe, it was possible something else had fallen apart. Ri had sleep-slipped them into an alternate reality that morning. Could these inconsistencies reveal residual changes he should sleep off? He craved alone time to think. First, though, he needed to keep his cool and play along with whatever whacked perception of reality his mother believed.

He giggled and pulled away from his mom's grip, staring at the lady cop. "Ah. Yes. My bad. Gotcha. Thanks."

Makena maintained a strained smile. She gripped her engraved silver belt buckle and tossed a polite nod. "You're welcome, son." She kicked forward a shiny boot with a matching silver tip.

Awkward silence. Janet—the fake human school counselor—spoke up. "Well, Anna. Should we start this?"

He took another step backward. His mom wore the "worried, but I'm tough and going to power through this" expression. A familiar look. He took a second to savor his mom exhibiting her face again and not a black ball of universal space. Her long auburn hair pulled behind her freckled face screamed worry. Her acting so distraught sent a wave of weakness down his limbs.

His mom forced her face to crack a smile. "Of course. Of course. Are you positive about not wanting any tea or coffee or something? I can make something, no trouble."

Janet smoothed out her skirt and rested her acrylic fingernails on her lap. "Please. I'm fine. This won't take us long. Hopefully." She leaned forward and peered at him above her spectacles.

His mom gestured at Makena. "You wanna come in and take a seat? This might take a few minutes."

"Protocol. Thanks." Makena held her intimidating cop stance in the open doorway. The sun started to set behind her.

His dry mouth and the pounding in his eardrums distracted him. He tasted the tension—saltine crackers choking him. His mom waved. "Please. Take your seat."

He obeyed, caught in the Librarian of Death's evil trance. The chair his mom had pulled from the kitchen cushioned his collapse. His throat failed to swallow the scratching dry crackers. "What's this about?"

His mom sighed. She tightened her lips.

Janet said, "Listen. Rieden. Your family has been through so much this past month and the last few years. Your mother is a brave, hard-working woman, do you agree?" Her fake kindness rattled his nerves.

"Yeah, sure. Of course."

Janet continued, "It's normal for children to act out when dealing with trauma. It's also normal for adults. Trauma is difficult for the human mind. No doubt, you've discussed this often with Esther, your therapist. Sometimes, though. Sometimes the mind is overwhelmed by the stress. Sometimes the pain goes so deep, the mind reacts in unpredictable and dangerous ways. Are you following me?"

Ri swayed, his attention spinning. No, the room started spinning. He discerned the importance of the counselor's words. His conscious self experienced an out-of-body sensation and floated from above. Watching himself, sitting and listening. The logic corresponded to zero sense.

Janet clutched her clipboard and squeezed it into her lap. "There's no easy way to disclose this. And we're not sure how much awareness you're having around what's happening. It's my opinion, and Esther's opinion, that you're experiencing what we call a psychotic break. A mental episode."

He floundered to dam up the tide of spasms crashing through his consciousness. "Sorry? A what? What nonsense am I hearing? Come out and say what you're saying, already!" he shouted, louder than intended. He hoped to avoid getting into even more trouble. All the tiptoeing riled him up.

His mom's vocal fry intensified. "Rieden, please. This is so hard on me. Try."

He studied her face. Pure pain. His skin felt hot, and the blood pumping through his body throbbed in his forehead. He fake coughed and gripped the two sides of the chair's seat, trying to stop the room from spinning. He enunciated through his clenched jaw. "What are you saying?"

Janet sighed and spoke even slower. So excruciating. "A psychotic break is when your mind can no longer distinguish between what is real and what is fantasy. Your mom tells me you've always had a vivid imagination. All this bad behavior. Cutting school. Getting into altercations with classmates and other children. Disappearing for hours and hours. Playing in abandoned buildings. Making a spectacle of yourself at the Sunshade Bar. Running away from the police officer who is striving to protect you. Destroying your room, the backyard, and not taking care of your personal hygiene. The cuts and scrapes on your arms and face. Is any of this sounding familiar?"

Ri instinctively smelled his armpit. He agreed it might have been a couple days since he showered. "Um. I guess."

It somewhat resembled his adventure. Except she was twisting the details. What did they remember during their time with black hole heads? Were their minds overflowing with strange stories and ridiculous ideas to fill in the gaps?

He locked down his body's trembling. While wiping his sweaty palms across his jeans, he drafted a quick reply. "Okay. A psychotic break. You're saying my brain isn't right. What trauma? Are you referring to my parents' divorce? Because that happened a few years ago. I'm over it. I miss Dad since he moved to Beijing for work. And sure, I'm bummed he doesn't call anymore. He's a super busy important person."

Janet's eyebrows lifted high. "And what else?"

What else? The only trauma he'd endured involved Rozul breaking his moon. And battling evil agents of death. What was she implying? "Um, okay. I'm guessing here. This broken trauma stuff you're mentioning is making me forget. What am I dealing with?"

His mom leaned forward. "Rieden. You've refused to say his name or talk about him for the past week. Your therapist finally admitted that during your last session, you talked as if he never existed. Why do you think we've all been so worried? You need to get this off your chest! Tell us what's going on inside your head. It's the only way..."

His mom trailed off, responding to Janet's extended hand.

"Rieden," said Janet. "Can you vocalize his name for us? Can you discuss him for a second? It's okay if it makes you cry."

His heart revved up again. What utter foolishness was this looney lady babbling? He shook his head and stared at his mom. "What? I'm so lost. What, what?"

His mom's eyes filled with tears. She placed her hands against her face and gasped. "He can't even say his name. I can't do this...."

Janet held up her hand again and whispered, "Please, Anna. Getting upset won't help him." She turned back to Ri and peered through her spectacles with wide eyes. "Rieden Reece. Please. Tell us your feelings.

Can you please discuss with us your twin brother, Robert? He's been a missing person for one month as of today."

34

The Obvious Obfuscation

T HE ROOM SPUN. Ri's awareness hit a brick wall. He tried to stand up but fell back into the chair. Time dripped through a leaky faucet, and cobwebs crawled across his face. He started hyperventilating. A twin brother? What tricks was this evil librarian conjuring up?

Ri collapsed. He stretched out his hand and used his bed to steady himself. His bed? He shook away his mental cobwebs and discovered himself on all fours crouching in his bedroom. How had he gotten here? His memory failed him.

A soft knock on the door. He pulled himself up onto his bed, sat on the edge, and faced his bedroom door. His mother, Anna, stood at the entrance, leaning on the door frame. She pulled frizzy strands from her wet face smothered with tears. Her freckles shined bright ruby. She whispered, "May I please come in?"

His consciousness drifted out of his body. The ultimate observer beholding reality from an elevated position. His mother's light ballerina feet tiptoed into the room. She gasped. Covering her mouth, she apologized with her hazel eyes. Her hand dropped and she sucked in a deep breath. A fragile smile cracked from beneath her pain. "May I sit?"

Ri peered around the room, searching for what had made his mother gasp. It was super messy, and he hadn't cleaned it in a few days. All his stuff lay strewn and cluttered. Why worry about cleaning? Fixing the universe came first.

His mom slid down beside him and rested on the bed. She slapped her hands on her thighs. "Well. You've been up to something here, mister."

Ri's desire to ask questions burned. This unfair reality pierced his heart. What made them babble on nonstop? A twin brother? Named Robert. A flash of memory slammed inside his awareness. Pictures. Movements. Emotions. A connection. He floundered to devise words to define the unfamiliar experience. "Uh. Mom. I'm a little confused. What's going on?"

She combed her trembling fingers through her matted hair. "Sweetie. Darling. I'm scared. And worried. I'm torn apart." She dropped her voice and leaned in a bit, whispering, "Please stay calm. I know your temper, Ri. We need to talk. Really talk. And I can't have you shouting and screaming when Janet and Makena are listening in the living room."

The intruders still occupied his house. He'd lost track of time. "How long have they been here?"

"For a bit. After you ran into the bedroom, I talked to them forever. Convinced them to let me come in and talk some...to let me try to reach you."

He longed for Rozul. If only he could reach out and touch his alien limbs, fill up on some alien-calm he shared. His heartbeat pulsed in rhythm, poised to pump a freight train speed at a split-second's notice. "Am I in trouble, Mom?"

She sighed. "What do you mean, trouble? You're worried someone's mad at you? Because no one is at all, honey. Everyone worries about you. We care about you. I love you. I hate to see you suffer."

The edges of his lips curled down. "Worried? Why is everyone worried?"

His mom chuckled. She caught herself and let out an extended sigh. "Because. You seem confused about what's happening."

He resisted his urge to shout, *I know exactly what is happening! I'm living the wrong reality! Rozul broke something else!* When his thoughts screamed, another flash of unfamiliar memories manifested. What did he remember? A twin brother? It tasted bittersweet.

He sighed and searched for an anchor of logic. He accepted a version of truth he could feed his mom until he found true answers. "Mom. I'm having trouble remembering stuff."

"Yes. I know, sweetie."

Ri shut his eyes tightly. He forced the foreign words through his clenched teeth: "Tell me about my missing brother."

His mom clamped her mouth shut. Tears welled in her eyes. She shook her head and released another frustrated laugh. "What do you want to know?"

"Why is he missing?"

Ri listened to the terrible story. A story full of pain and sadness his mother struggled to finish telling. Robert had gone missing a month ago. No word, no reason. Vanished. It devasted them. The town supported their search efforts. His mother mentioned many details. She spoke of news reports, school rallies, and the hospital fundraiser. She went on and on and on. Her voice resurrected ghostly memories infecting him to the core. Foreign thoughts arrived and saturated his soul. Did he remember his brother? This half of his whole. His protector. The smart, brave boy who always figured everything out and kept Ri's world sane. Forever living in his shadow.

His mom's bloodshot eyes burned into Ri. Her puffy eyes beamed through the creases. Her outstretched hand trembled, retrieving a box of tissues from the dresser top. A few dramatic dabs to her face, while she shuffled through the bedroom. She cleared her throat. "Oh no. You broke the mirror on your closet."

He glanced up absentmindedly, struggling to assemble the jumbled jigsaw pieces. A psychotic break? Or wrong reality? Both added up to zero sense. He shrugged. "Um. Don't remember how."

She squinted and stepped toward the mirror, her feet wading through piles of junk. Dumb old toys he never played with anymore. She lifted a photograph stuck into the top edge of the mirror frame. "You put Robert's picture right here. Why is his face scribbled out?"

Ri arose in a trance, mindlessly following his mother's lead. He reached for the picture. It looked familiar and curious and disturbing. A picture of Robert. Funny, he looked indistinguishable from Ri. He'd discerned the words "twin" and "brother." Identical twin never crossed his mind. The mysterious boy in the picture held up cotton candy on a stick. The other hand formed a peculiar two-finger sign. He shrugged. "Not sure."

His mom spun on her toes. She glanced at his aquarium between his window and closet. She stepped closer and leaned down, smirking. "Your frog's alive, of course. A five-star trooper all right. Sitting there on one of those mossy rocks, or green blobs, you boys call 'em. Do you remember when Robert decided to feed the fish ahead of time and dumped the entire bottle into the tank? All those poor guppies died. Your brave little frog survived, though it probably killed some of his brain cells. You two were young. Eight or nine. Have you fed your frog lately?"

He couldn't concoct a good guess. "Uh. No idea."

She shrugged. "Well, least we know he won't die." She lifted the bottle and sprinkled some flakes into the aquarium. She smiled to herself and almost wandered away, but she stopped short. She grunted. Stepping beside the tank, she reached up. A small toy tied to a string dangled from a hook in the ceiling. A goofy-looking doll or something. It hung upside down. She lifted it from the hook and pulled it in close. She rubbed the doll a bit, smoothing it out.

She held it up for him to examine. "You haven't played with this marionette in years. Why is it hanging upside down?"

Ri shrugged. "No clue." He reached out and took the marionette into his hands. A small wooden and plastic humanoid creature with a cue ball head. He rubbed the plastic creature in a habitual way. He didn't discern the meaning of the word etched into the forehead: *Luzor*. It whispered familiarity from a faraway, vague place. Ri strained for the missing memories. He asked, "What does this etching mean?"

His mom smirked. "Oh, you boys. Always creating a language and world of your own. Who's sure what happened, huh? You told me years ago, you and Rob fought. You got him wicked ticked. He etched the word 'loser' into your favorite puppet. Of course, he could never spell. Wrote it wrong. That's the longest you two ever went inflicting the silent treatment on each other. Ha!" She reached for the puppet and caressed its white glove, stroking it like a security blanket.

An odd sensation crawled all over Ri. The gravity in his room spun off balance. He seized the dresser top to steady himself. "Mom. Mom. I'm scared. I remember none of these things."

She tossed the marionette onto the bed and stepped forward, grabbing Ri's arms. "It's okay. I'm here. We can deal with this together."

New details unveiled themselves within his room. Next to his dresser, a skateboard covered with stickers leaned against the corner wall. Near the center of the skateboard, a picture of a capybara popped out. An unusual word. The word sprang into his brain along with a flash of memory. Robert's favorite animal. Capybara was an ugly giant rodent. Robert had grown obsessed with rats when they all lived with their dad in

Boston. Their apartment and the streets were infested with the rodents. He would chase the rats down the street on his skateboard. Robert's skateboard.

"Robert was an awesome athlete. He skateboarded. Right?"

His mom licked her lips and formed them into a straight line. She nodded, her eyes glistening. "Yep. He loved being the athlete. You're the brains and he's the muscle. Your protector and you felt safe in his shadow. Your words."

Ri kicked up a foolish grin. "He sounds cool."

His mom placed her hand over her heart and spun away. He turned away too, unable to distinguish between his own feelings and absorbing his mother's sadness. A snow globe containing a small figurine rested on the dresser. Next to it, a fishbowl of shiny rocks caught his interest.

He pointed. "What are these?"

His mom caressed the bowl with the care for a cherished heirloom. "Oh yeah! These are moon rocks. You bought them at the science museum down in San Diego. Do you remember? Same place you bought the snow globe." She stopped talking and peered down. She picked up a small black book sitting on a larger book. "My checkbook. This is what you used at the Sunshade Bar. I forgot I never shredded these."

His mom lifted the checkbook, and a book resting below it caught his attention. A library book with the title *Emergency Preparation for Disasters*. It seemed familiar. Why? The memory eluded him. She followed his gaze. She formed a half frown. "Yeah. Robert's last library book. He checked it out for a report. I haven't had the heart to return it." She chuckled—with layered pain buried beneath. "Ah. He picked it because he wanted to bore the teacher to death. That's something Robert would say."

Ri dropped his chin. The conversation. The foreign memories. His temples throbbed. His heartbeat pounded in the distance. He flopped back onto his bed. This reality burned bright. Familiar. It spoke a form of difficult truth. Was it his truth? His reality? Or had Rozul messed up, hardcore?

His mom sat on the bed. "You okay, honey?"

He shook his head in slow motion. "No. No. No. Not okay. None of this is making sense. I remember nothing. It comes from someplace far away in a dream. It sounds wonderful. Yet, at the same time, terrible. Robert...is...missing?"

His mom stopped breathing. She gripped the mattress with trembling arms. She coughed and forced out shallow rips of air. "Listen. Son. There's a lot on our plate. We've got big problems. Bigger problems than our minds can handle. On top of that, we also have choices. Choices about how we respond to our problems. You need to make a choice."

He knitted his eyebrows. "A choice? What do you mean? What choice?"

She rested her palms on her thighs and dove deep down into Ri's soul. "The counselor. Your therapist. The school. The police. They all want to take you away from me. They want to commit you to a psychiatric hospital for your psychotic break with reality."

35

The Calm Contemplation

R I STAGGERED BACKWARD AND crashed into his dresser. The room turned upside down. Manifested words twisted and slithered, loud and echoing. They encircled him with the tenacity of hungry vultures. Crazy. Psychotic. Weirdo. Freak. Oddball. Stupid.

A memory surfaced of his brother Robert screaming at him the night he went missing. Ri collapsed, and his mom rushed to his side.

"Ri! Rieden! What's wrong, honey? I'm not trying to upset you. Listen. Please, I know this is hard. You must be brave. You must be strong. Please. Or they'll separate what's left of our family."

She held his hand with a tender grip and helped him sit back on the bed. His mom's words echoed down a distant tunnel. Weakness consumed him. Powerless. Defeated. He feared losing this connection more than battling all the evil in the universe. Brave. Ri was brave. No, Robert was brave. But Robert was gone, so now it was his turn to act brave. His breathing slowed and his arms tingled.

He peered up with wide eyes and a gaping mouth. "Mom. Please don't let them take me away."

She leaned in and hugged him tight, tears streaming down her cheeks. She pushed her face against his forehead and whispered, "I won't, honey. I won't. You're safer here with me. You just need to be strong for a minute. Convince Janet and Makena that you aren't a threat to others and yourself. Tell them you remember Robert and are sad and confused, that's all. They want you safe. We all do. You can sit and cry in your room all night, later. For a New York minute, you need to be strong."

He curled up a wry lip. "I'm not gonna cry, Mom."

His mom chuckled. "There's my strong boy. You always hated crying."

"Crying is for losers."

She scrunched up her mouth into a smile-frown. She ruffled his messy mop and shrugged her shoulders. "Does this mean you'll be okay? You're not lying to me to protect me? We're discussing you. I'm devasted. It's impossible to hide my pain from you. I miss Robert so much it makes my body ache all day long. The thought of losing you, too? No suh. How much can a mother take...." She paused and choked back another flood of tears. "Listen. Listen to me. I'm not worried about me. It's what's best for you. I know you. I know your unstoppable brilliance. You loved Robert so much; you worried about him day and night. You always gave him a hard time even though you couldn't live without him. This is your way of coping. You'll be okay. You just need time to process the loss of the other half of your whole. We need each other. This is our new normal. In the long run, I don't see how taking you away from me is going to make you any better."

He listened to her speech, a detached foreign language from another dimension. He understood. She seemed to speak of someone else. He did remember. Bits and pieces. Snags of conversations. The affection he carried for Robert. The anguish of him disappearing into the night. Blaming himself. Feeling an intense duty to fix it. He itched to help find his brother. The thoughts and emotions swirled. He stared into a washing machine and caught faint glimpses of his own belongings.

His memories. He balked at his mom smothering him. It made him feel childish and awkward. Yet, nothing else made sense.

He hugged his mom back and squeezed her tight. "Please don't let them send me to the crazy ward."

His mom let out a deep sigh. "They won't. I can give you a moment. Can you be strong? Can you tell them what they need to hear so they can trust us?"

Ri formed a crooked smirk. She stood up and tiptoed to the doorway. She turned around and gazed back. His heart ached, having missed his mother's caring eyes protecting him the way she did. She plucked another tissue off the dresser and wiped away more tears. After stuffing the tissue into her front pocket, she straightened her scrubs and stood upright and walked away.

He sat motionless and waited.

Eventually, his mom called for him. He obediently marched into the living room to face the evil Librarian of Death. The alien monster concealed in human form. He lied. He claimed no confusion, told her he missed his brother Robert. He promised to listen to his mother no matter what. Makena remained silent, guarding, watching, and listening from the open door. Janet asked the same questions again and again and again. He kept his heartbeat steady. *Stay calm*, he told himself. He suppressed his churning anger. He simply lied, again and again and again.

Twenty minutes later, they left. Ri had convinced the adults they could put away the straitjacket.

Channeling the strength he'd used to conquer the evil taking over the universe, he gazed up at his mom. "May I go to my room? I gotta clean it."

She sat at the dining room table, sipping her tea. Her left hand trembled. She stared off into space. He approached her and placed his hand on her arm. "Are you okay, Mom?"

Her eyelids fluttered and she snapped out of her trance. "I should be asking you that, not the other way around."

"Come on. They're gone. Tell me the truth."

His mom held the tea close to her mouth, the steam swirling and rolling through wisps of her hair. Her head quivered and her body shivered. "I'm fine. Forget cleaning your room tonight. There's another day of school tomorrow. Get some sleep."

The strength of a thousand stars fueled his force of will as he reassured his mom, "We'll find my brother."

She set the teacup down hard, her hands trembling more. She opened her mouth to speak only to clamp it shut again. She dropped her head and stared at her lap for a few seconds. Lifting her heavy head, she forced one last smile. "I hope so too, Rieden."

His mom lied to him. She was why he'd learned to lie so well himself. He offered no help by forcing her to think on topics she avoided. She had her victory for the day. She'd saved Ri. He grinned. "Thanks, Mom. Sorry for my confusion. I'm okay now. You helped me. I'm gonna clean some of my room tonight so there's not so much to do tomorrow. Gonna have a bunch of extra homework to do."

He hurried away, not wanting to decipher his mom's micro-expressions. The despair might unravel the fake calm he was channeling. He shuffled his feet to his room, and his mom called out weakly, "Goodnight moon."

He closed his bedroom door. In a mindless, robotic motion, he cleaned up his room. He lifted the disarrayed toys and dropped them back into the box. While he shuffled around the room, flashes of new memories surfaced. Toys and stuff in his room intermingling with his universal adventure. Skewed splinters of reality explaining different versions of his adventures. He found a moon rock inside his frog's tank. He lifted it out and placed it back in the pile with the others. Something sparkled within the snow globe. Lifting it, he examined the tiny sticker of a superhero attached to the backside of the snow globe. When viewed from the front, the sticker superhero appeared imprisoned.

He found his night-light ripped from the wall. He picked up the light—in the shape of a five-pointed star—and reinserted it into the outlet next to his closet. He hadn't used his nightlight in ages. Tonight. Tonight, his stomach churned. No Rozul hiding in his closet. No adventure to distract him from the knowledge of his missing brother.

His energy drifted away. Lifting strewn objects off his floor became a heavy chore. He could finish cleaning in the morning. He crawled into bed and lay on top of the covers. The cracked-open window allowed the warm night breeze to crawl inside. The stars burned bright. No visible moon, at least not through the window's view.

He sighed. A panic surge so powerful it knocked him numb. He visualized his brother, Robert. He remembered him. He'd never imagined life without him. Born minutes apart. They spent every waking minute together. They did everything together. A year ago, his mother had moved them into this house so they could have separate rooms. It had resurfaced his parent's divorce all over again. He'd never shared his feelings on the matter, never wanting to seem like a weakling for admitting the truth. But the truth was, Ri missed talking to him at night and falling asleep midway through concocting their adventures.

Part of him itched to ruminate on memories with Rob. The other part protected him from overwhelming pain. He searched for his sheep. Strange. He found the sheep, sitting near the stream, collapsed. They lay on their backs in the grass and sucked on lollipops. They had gathered the wood from the fence and lit a big bonfire. When they discerned Ri asking to count for him, they pretended they couldn't see him. They waved dismissive hooves and rolled their heads backward as if life were a grand chore.

He grunted and shoved his arms under his pillow. The nightlight glowed near his feet, a soft, lonesome star in a dark sky. Life would go on. It would continue. He would continue to live. But what about his reality? Would he wake up and discover he never had a brother? That he remained in the wrong reality, and in this reality, the Ri's life he occupied had a twin brother? Or worse, what about when he woke up tomorrow? Would his reality reveal his lost sanity? His adventure nothing more than a fabricated delusion? That they should've hauled his butt off in the paddy wagon and hooked up his brain to electrodes?

What was reality? Could he even choose? Did he possess the capacity to create his own reality, or was it thrust upon him by the corrupt universe?

What reality could he return to, now that he knew about his twin brother whom he loved more than life and missed terribly? Would he forget again? Would forgetting feel better? What if Robert was still alive, somewhere out in the world, and Rieden had failed to find him? What if he lay captured, hurt, unconscious, or something worse? And Ri had given up?

Why was reality so painful?

His thoughts raced with frenetic madness. They circled and circled. *Sleep.* His exhausted body cried out for sleep. *Sleep, please.* In the morning, he would think clearer.

But morning burned a million light-years away.

36

The Bright Beginning

R I'S LASHES FLUTTERED. AWARENESS dropped a heavy weight onto his chest. Light. Bright light. Too bright. He shouldn't have tried to sleep with the night-light on. A cackling hyena disturbed his attempt at slumber. The cackling echoed from the Einstein clock far away in an alternate reality.

He lifted his torso and examined the dark room. Except, the darkness vanished. A light from outside poured through his window. He gazed up. The moon! Brighter than he had ever seen it before. Brighter than the night Rozul broke it. The full moon hovered: blue, brilliant, and beautiful. He yawned. He had managed to fall asleep and was now wide-awake at midnight. The moon blazed so strong it warmed his skin.

A soft rapping came at the window.

A branch rubbed against his window, though no trees grew close to his room. The wind stayed silent. He ripped off his covers and dropped his feet to the cold ground. He lifted the window wide open and stuck his head out. He wasn't afraid. *Break again, moon! Come on, do something! What's happening?*

The memory of the limb scratching clicked into place. Rob. Rob used to creep to his window at night. Sometimes they would sneak into the doghouse to finish their conversation. Or to plan something cool to do at school the next day. Rob always overflowed with so many ideas. Ri struggled to keep him in line sometimes. Often, he would go along with it because he found it so difficult to say no to Rob.

The crickets chirped. The toads growled. A coyote called in the distance. The moisture in the air tickled his nose. He expected to find Rob crouching below his window. But no one was there. Only a normal lot with a humongous glowing moon hanging from the sky.

He whispered at the moon, "Are you real, Rozul? Did I dream everything? Is my mind cracked? Did I miss Rob so much I dreamt up an alternate reality?" Tears welled up. Only losers cried. Crying solved nothing. Nobody could see him now, though. Only the bright and beautiful moon glowing a magnificent color only for him. He gave up the fight and allowed the burning acid to drip down his cheeks. Why did crying frighten him?

He could crawl back into bed. The sweetness of sleep sang softly to him. If his brain was broken, he needed to fix it. He couldn't fix his brain if he couldn't trust it to differentiate reality from fantasy. What would Rob say if he were here?

"Look at the facts, bro. Why's the moon so bright? You're taking stuff for granted. Analyze that. Does the bright moon make sense?"

He admired the amazing wonder. The flowing blue light pulsated and calmed him. Did some part of him not want to face his unwanted reality? Could his brain break so badly it conjured imaginary things? He'd read lots of stories about deranged people. Losing his mind equaled losing completely. He trusted his mind. His mind meant everything.

He had lost Rob. And Rob meant everything.

Another sound. A buzzing. Probably his phone vibrating. His mom didn't let him keep his phone in his room at night. Unless she'd forgotten tonight. The soft buzzing continued. For sure, a metal object tapping wood. An insect?

He peeled himself away from the mesmerizing sight. The light from the moon mixed with the soft glow of his night-light helped him discern the contents of his room. Still messy, though no longer at DEFCON One for disaster. The buzzing grew louder. The mindfulness section of his brain observed a new reaction—his heart beat steady. The hairs on his arms rested. He remained at complete calm. Was this your life when you were nuts? No longer afraid of new threats? He followed the noise to his dresser.

The pen. The pen Rozul had given him. The golden pen with the silver tip. It vibrated against the dresser top. Reminded him of Morse code. Faint. Buzz. Buzz, buzz. Buzz. Inside the pen's top, a dim red light pulsed. It longed for a push. You always push the glowing red button.

Ri pushed it.

The color flipped to bright green, and the pen jumped. He shielded his eyes, thinking it might explode. No. Not an explosion. The pen jumped to life with sentient determination. An angry dragon fly darting around his room. It discovered Shelly's sticker book resting on a stack of debris. The pen started writing of its own accord. It jotted down words with rapid electrical pulses dancing up and down the length of the pen.

He held his forehead with both hands and stared. His heartbeat remained steady. His breathing rhythm stayed normal. Was this how you lost your mind? Giving in to hallucinations? Should he find his camera? Even if he used his Canon to capture snapshots, who would believe him? CGI and special effects made this nothing more than child's play, pun intended. *Ugh! Puns...* Now that he remembered Rob, he recalled all the ridiculous things Rob would say on purpose to dig under Ri's skin.

The pen collapsed, the green light pulsing. It waited for him. Tempted him. Taunted him. Come closer, you cannot resist the reading of this note....

He gulped and clenched his fists. Should he explode with anger? What was the proper reaction to losing one's mind? If alternate realities did occur, could there exist a place where everyone had lost their mind and they all fit in?

Had everyone else lost their mind, and he was the only sane one left?

Curiosity, a burning desire burrowing through his skin, overpowered his limbs. He stepped forward in a trance, mesmerized by the words written in the sticker book. He picked it up from the pile. Rushing to the window, he lifted the open pages under the bright moonlight. The pen acted smart. It had found a page with removed stickers. It wrote with standard ink on the rough surface. It burned the letters into the smooth wax of the empty shapes. He read the message:

Dear Rieden,

It's been a minute. Yup. You're torqued at me, for sure. So glad I'm not there to see Mom. Always the drama queen. No worries, time is the master fixer. Aw, Reek. I sure wish you could see things from my perspective. It's amazing. Sure, yeah, I've got a lot of explaining to do. In time. We'll get there. I'm reaching out to you because this is a pivotal moment in your current path. You make some bad moves, and it alters your future drastically. Technically, I shouldn't tell you so much. First, I seldom follow the rules. Second, you always bombard me with a billion plus one questions, so I'm getting us straight to the point.

You're not cracking up, bro. I'm still alive. Our adventure hasn't even started yet.

The alien you call Rozul made a mess. He did me a solid favor and that's why I helped him get his sister back. It's too much to explain in a quick note, but let's leave it at: I'm super new at this inter-universal translation fenomenon (Yes, wipe your smug look off your face, I've got no clue how to spell "phenomenon." Most universes scrapped old-school written words.

I digress.) The point is, I thought he'd have plenty of time. Explain my activities to you while you helped him find his sister. The transfer signal got hacked and he thrust his star will into your toy. Broken moons. Lost memories. Muddled powers. I watched the playback, totally ugly. Yadda, yadda, yadda. You lived through it, sure, sure. I'm a bit lost without you too, I'll say it out loud. Oh, yeah, this note will self-destruct after you read it. I've always wanted to do that.

So. Next steps. Wait for my signal. And bro, I'm serious, keep my secret from Mom. She's unable to handle anything besides needles. I could fly down in a spaceship and hover over to her doorstep with anti-grav boots, and she'd only comment on the smudge of chocolate on my cheek. Moms. Whatcha gonna do?

I'll make real contact soon. At first my associates blocked me from bringing you on board. But after you smacked those two claw-brains around, my associates started to see your value. You and I, we got the same genes. The same brain. We focus on different things. That makes us a formidable team. Time to unleash our twin power.

Okay. See you soon, bro. Love ya, yadda, yadda, yadda.

Robert Reece

P.S. Time to look up.

Ri stopped reading and gazed at the moon. The glowing orb beamed so bright he could hardly behold it. He discovered something else. A hand. And then an arm and a hand. A shadow crawled across the moon. The moon stayed intact—he recognized the oddly shaped alien Rozul waving at him.

Next to Rozul, another shadow emerged. Smaller and familiar too. Robert. Robert and Rozul's shadows waved to him, clutching the sides of the moon like it was a spaceship hovering above Earth.

They stopped waving. The moon disappeared and winked out of existence, leaving behind a starless sky. His hands burned too hot. The sticker book ignited on fire, though not with the type of combustion able to burn him. The atoms transformed into heat and light. The clear flames licked upward with cool steam rolling away from boiling water.

The sticker book disappeared. The moon disappeared. He stood with his mouth wide open. Thinking. Thinking. Thinking. So many new thoughts. So many new questions. So many wonderfully terrifying emotions bubbling inside. He wasn't crazy. He was saner than most. He could distinguish between reality and his imagination. His brother was alive! And they had a million more adventures to go on.

Right?

Acknowledgments

The list of people who I wish to extend my gratitude and appreciation to is lengthier than my novel. My path to publication took a couple extra decades longer than planned. But such is the nature of life. My path twisted and turned in ways I never imagined, and yet it is the only path I could have taken. I'm grateful to have accomplished my lifelong dream. And I aim to inspire my readers to also make their dreams come true. In the meantime, I thank my readers, present and future, for bringing my vision to life in your imagination.

Along the way I interacted with hundreds of authors, editors, agents and supporters. Some, I remember their names. Some, only their smiling faces. My teachers. My bosses. The random stranger who, when I mentioned I was writing a book, their eyes lit up like I had handed them a thousand-dollar bill. Giving yourself permission to call yourself an author is an honor and a privilege. Storytelling is in the human DNA. It is how we perceive the world and understand it. That is why most people have a book they've never written but have thought about often. We live, love, and experience our realities through metaphor and story. And we cherish those who succeed at telling theirs.

Modern civilization humbles me. Humanity still must take tremendous strides forward to mature into emotional health. Yet, the technology humanity has willed into being is breathtaking. The advancement of technology has accelerated for the last six hundred years, beginning with the printing press. Without this technology, I would only have a few people to tell my stories to. I would be stumbling around carrying my dry and crinkled scrolls. Hoping for a glimmer of understanding from random strangers. Wondering if those unsuspecting souls understood the fantastical ideas my brain concocted. With modern technology, we can proclaim our stories across the globe. And discover our precious audience.

Internet. Google. YouTube. Amazon. Podcasts. Laptops. Smart Phones. I could list a thousand more bits of tech right down to the binary code. A code a human dreamt into existence. And then convinced others to invent a language via numbers to layer our lives on top of it. Without these inventions, and the free education provided by so many generous people, I would have not made it this far. And have no means to share my stories with the world. For this, I express my deep gratitude from the depth of my bones.

My editor, Stephanie Slagle, is beyond amazing. She brought my story to life and infused it with incredible power. Her kindness, brilliance and terrific insights are invaluable. My book cover designer and illustrator, Kim Dingwall, is awesome. The moment I discovered her work, I fell in love with her style. She is the perfect fit for Rieden Reece. She lifted the words from the page with great care. And she breathed the heart of his struggles into beautiful artwork. Thank you both, so much.

My family and friends are marvelous. A grand privilege I have—blessed with so many. For too many years, I believed in error others held me back and created "resistance." In his book The War of

Art Steven Pressfield exposes this painful truth with clever wit. The only "resistance" I experienced was the fear and anxiety created within me. The moment came where I stopped asking others for permission and made up my own mind to do what I needed to do. When I did, every single friend and family member supported me a 150%. It both surprised me and humbled me. At our best, humans want other humans to succeed. And all my family and friends are simply the best.

At the top of the list of people I must thank for helping me, is my dear mother. She has with consistent steadiness been an inspiration my entire life. Every step of my journey, she cheered, supported, and helped me. She did everything in her power to show she believed in me. Not every son receives such a gift. I am often overwhelmed by this gift.

Matt Guzman is somewhat spoiled. The residents of beautiful San Diego, CA allow him to live there, and they barely complain about it. After managing restaurants for twenty years, he made a drastic decision. Quit. And use everything he learned the hard way about leadership and communication to help children. He's obsessed with emotional health and storytelling. Combining these two passions, Matt crafts sci-fi stories for his twelve-year-old self—still hiding inside his adult brain. He once won an honorable mention from the Writers of the Future Contest. That went straight to his head and now there's no stopping him.

Would you please write me a book review?
I love feedback from my readers! Writing a
review is one of the best ways to help me
reach more readers like you.

AMAZON

GOODREADS

Would you do me a HUGE favor and sign up
for my Mindfast newsletter?
Be the first to get exclusive content
designed for storytellers and readers.
Contests, discounts, sneak peeks, and more!

https://authormattguzman.com/

https://www.amazon.com/author/mattguzman

https://www.goodreads.com/authormattguzman

COMING SOON!

COMING SOON!

Riaden Reece and the Final Flower
June 2023

Riaden Reece and the Scroll of Life
Jan 2024

Riaden Reece and the Water World
June 2024

Riaden Reece and the Virtual Girl
Jan 2025

Riaden Reece and the Dark Shadow
June 2025

Riaden Reece and the End Game
Jan 2026

Connect with Matt

Website

Instagram

Facebook

Twitter

www.authormattguzman.com

www.instagram.com/authormattguzman

www.facebook.com/MattDahGooz

www.twitter.com/AuthorMattGuz